FERAL IS THE BEAST

CURSED CAPTORS
BOOK TWO

FERAL IS THE BEAST

NISHA J. TULI

FERAL IS THE BEAST

Copyright © 2024 by Nisha J Tuli

All rights reserved. No part of this book may be used or reproduced in any manner whatsoever without written permission except in the case of brief quotations used in critical articles or reviews. This book is a work of fiction. Names, characters, businesses, organizations, places, events, and incidents either are the product of the author's imagination or are used fictitiously. Any resemblance to actual persons, living or dead, events, or locales is entirely coincidental.

For information contact : http://www.nishajtuli.com/

Cover design by Saint Jupiter

ISBN: 978-1-990898-15-0

First Edition: March 2024

10 9 8 7 6 5 4 3 2

For all the morally grey heroines and the ones who appreciate them.

Chapter One

"Oh *fuck*, that hurts," Savryn hisses, his head dropping back and his eyes squeezing hard enough to force tears from the corners. "Sometimes, I think you take pleasure in making me suffer."

With my tongue wedged between my teeth, I dig my thin silver needle into the firm meat of his pectoral, perhaps with a smidge more force than necessary.

"My sweet Sav, I have no idea what you mean," I coo, gracing him with a faux-innocent smile before I pull out the instrument and dig it in again, twisting just a little.

"Ves."

He grunts out my name as his hands tighten around my hips, where I'm straddling him in my custom-designed tattoo chair. Upholstered in supple black leather, it's just barely long enough to accommodate

Savryn's six-foot-four frame. A lever allows me to adjust it to the correct angle, and it is currently cocked at thirty degrees as I work on a section of his chest.

"Fuuuuuck," Savryn groans again, and I roll my eyes because, really, he's just a big baby.

I tuck back a lock of my dark hair and exhale a wicked laugh as I wipe away a drop of blood beading on the surface of his smooth, tanned skin.

Savryn is so very pretty to look at. All golden muscle and dark blond hair just begging your fingers to run through it.

The man also doesn't have two brain cells to rub together. But that's okay. He's my favorite type of lover. Not all that bright, but definitely sexy. I don't need anyone suffering from delusions of controlling me or telling me what to do. The 'smart' ones think every dull thought conjured from the recesses of their pea-sized brains is worth listening to, and that usually couldn't be further from the truth.

"Stop complaining," I say. "You wanted this one to be strong, so it needs more magic."

A pained grunt is his answer as his eyes squeeze shut again, his forehead creasing with tension.

I select a different needle from my small side table and dip it into a vial of ink spelled for strength. Savryn is a hunter, providing a steady supply of meat for the local butcher, but the forests around here are dangerous for mortal men.

Within its leafy shadows, one can expect to find the typical bears and wildcats to contend with, but also far more sinister things. Demons that roam the darkness of the woods, supposedly guarding the barrier to the Shadow Realm. I'm not sure how true that last part is, but it certainly makes for a good story told around the fire at night.

Regardless, they're incredibly vicious and can easily overpower any human.

After the last time I ran from my life, I settled here to set up my shop, figuring the presence of monsters would draw fewer eyes my way. When you're constantly distracted by a distant threat, it's easy to overlook the one living in your midst.

Savryn isn't afraid of me, though. He knows what I am and comes to me for protection with my special—but entirely secret from everyone else—gifts.

He grits his teeth as I pierce a row of dark marks around his dusky nipple that form the mouth of a demon, the rest of its body flowing down his ribs. We've done this countless times before. As he uses the protection of my magic, they fade over time, necessitating regular maintenance.

Unfortunately, the dramatic whining is part of the ritual, too.

"Shut up," I say, rolling my hips in a way that makes him whimper. "Does that make it better, my baby?" I ask, cupping his cheek and thrusting out my bottom lip.

Another requirement in our twisted little ritual is the absence of underwear under my skirt. The thick length of his *incredibly* impressive cock hardens between my thighs as he holds me down and rubs himself against me firmly enough to make my stomach flutter.

He's right that I get pleasure from hurting him, but he gets pleasure from it too.

When I'm done with the section around his nipple, I lean down and flick my tongue against the peak, pulling out an agonized groan.

"That's my good boy," I say, and he rewards me with a dazzling smile. The one that convinced me to let him into my bed in the first place. "We're almost done."

He nods and then squeezes my hips again as I tend to the other side of his chest. His fingers are going to leave bruises on the soft flesh around my waist, but I don't really mind. There's something enticing about him marking me like this. It's not permanent—they'll fade away, and no one will ever know he was there—but for a short time, I like the idea of him wanting me so much that it leaves physical proof.

Before I stick the needle in again, I reach between us and unlace his breeches. Savryn grins because it's the signal that I'm nearly finished with my work tonight.

I settle back, gasping at the heat of his scalding cock against my already-wet pussy. I take a moment to stroke myself against him, rubbing my clit before I lean down and continue working, adding another swirling line across the flat plane of his hard right pectoral. This one will improve his hearing, making it difficult for anything to creep up on him in the forest.

"There," I say, depositing the needle back onto the tray and wiping my hands.

I've barely let go, but he's already pulling me towards him, his hand cupping the back of my neck as he swirls his hips in a way that has my head falling against him with a breathless moan.

"Thank fuck," he mumbles into my shoulder, shifting us so the head of his cock is positioned at my entrance. I've fucked Savryn more times in this chair than I can count. The bolts squeak, reminding me they'll need tightening soon.

Savryn's cock slides into me, parting my slick flesh, and I gasp at the fullness of his width. He thrusts up with force, and goddess, this is always the best part. My fingers dig into his shoulders as I ride his hips, reveling in my pleasure—that is, until the jingle of bells blasts through the haze of my lust, grinding us both into stillness. Someone is at the front door of my shop.

"What the hell?" I say. "I'm sure I locked it."

I slide off Savryn and smooth down my skirt, an uncomfortable premonition ticking at the back of my neck.

Savryn stands up too, his large hands already curling into fists.

"Stay here," I say as I open the door before I head

down the short hall to another door that leads into my apothecary. No one else knows what goes on in my back room with Savryn, and I want to keep it that way. I guard my secrets closely. I gave up the magical tattoo trade decades ago when I'd had enough of…well, everything.

I push open the swinging door while straightening my top, hoping I don't look too debauched.

"Hello?" I call as I enter the main area of my store.

To most people living in Twilight's End, my apothecary is a place to come for herbs and tinctures for common viruses and illnesses. I imbibe everything with just a pinch of magic to ensure it works well enough so they keep returning for more but not enough for anyone to think I'm capable of miracles. I am, but that's knowledge I keep to myself. People expect too much when they believe you can solve all of their problems.

A man stands on the far side of the room, facing a large cabinet, where he studies the vials and jars I offer up for sale. My shop turns a tidy enough profit to keep me more than comfortable. Of all the shit-hole towns I've found myself in over the centuries, Twilight's End ranks in the top two or three. I don't even consider it a shit-hole. Mostly, it's quite lovely, minus the man-eating demons in the forest and the vicious Feral King who rules over this dominion.

As long as both parties leave me alone, I'm more than content to enjoy my quiet existence.

"Can I help you?" I look at the door, wondering how

this stranger got in. I must have forgotten to lock it, though that's not really like me. Besides, everyone who lives in Twilight's End knows I'm closed at this time of night.

The man turns slowly, and I can instantly see he isn't a local. He's probably in his late thirties, with a head of shaggy dark hair that looks like it could use a trim. He's dressed finely enough, though the clothes don't seem to fit him very well.

"Vespera Foxhollow?" he asks, tipping his head and staring at me in a way I really don't care for.

"Who's asking?" I plant my hands on my hips, wondering if Savryn is listening in case I need backup. While I could use magic to flatten this son of a bitch, I prefer not to let anyone witness what I'm capable of.

The man's face stretches into a smile. "An interested party."

"I don't know what that's supposed to mean."

I don't even try to keep the irritation out of my voice. Just what I needed tonight was some asshole coming in here with his cryptic demands, interrupting what was about to be a very good orgasm.

"My master is interested in you. He has a proposal."

"Who is your master?"

"I can't tell you that. But if you'll come with me, he'll make it worth your while."

I snort at that. "You expect me to pick up and follow

some strange man who barged into my *locked* shop late at night?"

He grins, showing off white teeth except for a gold one in the front.

"Smart girl."

Girl. I inhale a deep breath, resisting the urge to smack him across the face—I'm old enough to be his great, great, great grandmother—but decide what I really want is to get him out of here so I can return to my previous entertainment.

"It's about your skills," he says, dragging out the 's' with a hiss that makes my blood turn icy.

"If your master needs a cure for an illness, then please come back tomorrow with a list of symptoms, and I'll see what I can put together for you. For now, my shop is closed."

The stranger raises an eyebrow and scans the store, acting like he's not all that impressed with what he sees before he makes a tutting noise.

"Come, *Vespera*. You know that's not what I mean. My master is interested in what you can *really* do."

I resist the urge to step back, worried it will reveal my guilt.

"I don't know what you're talking about," I say, marching towards the door and opening it. "As I said, I'm closed now."

The man's insipid grin remains as he scans my apothecary one more time, stretching up onto one foot, trying to get a peek past the swinging doors that lead to the back.

I grip the door handle, doing my best to stay where I am and not walk over to wrap my hands around his neck. I'm just a simple village healer with a knack for finding the right concoctions. I plaster on a bland smile as he turns towards me and saunters closer, his thumbs tucked into his belt loops like a complete idiot.

When he reaches the door, he offers me a tip of his imaginary hat. "I must've gotten the wrong witch then."

I try not to react to those pointed words.

"Indeed," is all I say.

"Sorry to have disturbed you," he says, though it's obvious he's not sorry at all. I give him a tight nod.

Then he finally steps through the door, and I slam it behind him, securing the lock before I finally allow myself to breathe.

Chapter Two

After the stranger leaves, I stand with my back pressed to the door, waiting for my heart to settle in my chest. Who the fuck was that? I spin around and lift the corner of the curtain, peering out into the street to ensure he's gone. The streetlamps provide enough illumination to show it's empty and that he's no longer outside.

Still, I keep watching, peering down the road until my gaze finds the gloomy stone castle sitting on top of a cliff overlooking the valley cradling Twilight's End. A giant skull carved into the rock is the mark of the Feral King, who rules over these lands. Famously known for transforming into a beast at night, preying on the nearby villages and, more importantly, their wretched inhabitants. He's a monster who keeps everyone in his kingdom living on the edge of fear, worried they'll become the next bit of sinew he uses to floss his teeth. Every king I've ever known is the same, seizing power through violence and intimidation to compensate for a lack of assets in other departments.

I drop the curtain and squeeze my eyes shut.

"Vespera?" A deep male voice blasts through my panic, and I scream, jumping up and spinning around.

"Goddess!" I shout at Savryn, who's standing in the swinging doorway, shirtless with his pants still unlaced. "You scared me."

"Sorry," he says, his pretty face screwing into concern. "Are you okay? What happened?"

"Nothing," I say, checking the lock again and then once more for good measure. I touch the concealed tattoo on the top of my hand and flick out my fingers, murmuring a few words to erect a barricade. This isn't a precaution I bother with most of the time—the folk in this town are simple people who know not to mess with my shop, but tonight, I crave the added layer of protection.

No one could have found me out.

I gave up that life for a reason, and I never want to return.

Turning to the window for another look, I peer outside, seeing nothing else amiss. Once again, my gaze finds the Feral King's castle, perched on its cliff like a sentient gargoyle. Normally its ominous presence does little to move me, but tonight, it makes something itchy crawl down the back of my dress, a shiver rippling through my limbs. That man spooked me tonight.

A pair of warm arms circle me from behind.

"Come on," Savryn murmurs, dragging me back. "We weren't done yet."

I turn around and bite my lip, scanning my shop, searching for anything that seems out of place. I'm *sure* I locked the door when I closed up earlier.

"Vespera," Savryn says in a sing-song voice. "Where did you go?"

I look up at him, wrapping my hands around his biceps, attempting to summon a smile. "I'm fine. Sorry. It's nothing."

"You sure? You look a little pale."

"I'm sure." I nod and then loop my arms around his neck to pull him down for a kiss.

Though I'm of average height, he makes me feel like a tiny forest sprite. This is how I like them: big and pretty, and not much else.

He groans as he nuzzles my neck, and I try to slip into the mood again, but my thoughts keep wandering back to that strange man, wondering what he wanted. Who was his master, and how did he know what I was? What do either of them want from me? How could they have tracked me down? I've been so careful to leave behind every last thread of my old life.

"Ves," Savryn mumbles. "You're thinking too hard. I can practically hear it."

I let out a huff. "Well, one of us has to."

Savryn grins and then pushes me back until I bump against the counter.

"Let me take your mind off it," he says, and I appreciate that he doesn't ask me any more questions or try to pry into places I don't want him. Good, simple Savryn.

With his huge hands, he lifts me onto the counter. "I know how to make those gorgeous brown eyes roll into the back of your head."

He's not wrong, I think to myself as he slides his hands up my calves and then my knees, pushing up my skirt until it's bunched around my waist. He parts my thighs until I'm spread open for him before he drops to his knees, proceeding to eat me out with unrelenting enthusiasm. For a few moments, I let myself sink into it, allowing his very skillful tongue and fingers to work their magic until he makes me come so hard that I scrape a set of gouges into my pristine wooden countertop.

When he's done, he laps me up like an eager puppy, climbs up my body, and kisses me so I can taste the salt of my arousal.

"Better?" he asks with a hopeful look in his eyes.

"Much," I lie.

Sure, that was very enjoyable, but I'm still thinking about the stranger who interrupted my evening. Savryn frowns.

"I can go," he says, and that's another thing I love

about him—he never takes it personally when I want him out of my hair.

"Thanks," I say. "I'm sorry. I think I'm just tired."

"No problem. I'll see you tomorrow." He pecks me on the cheek before he strides away, exiting through the swinging door while I enjoy the view of his perfect, leather-clad ass.

I hear him gathering his things before the back door opens and then closes. As soon as he's gone, I hurry through my shop and lock that one, too. When I start cleaning up, I notice Savryn has left his bow behind. He'll need it first thing in the morning. I know he likes to leave at dawn to get a jump on the geese that paddle around the pond.

I grab it and swing the door open.

"Savryn!" I call, stepping into the alley. "You forgot your bow!"

Suddenly, darkness obscures my vision as the drag of rough fabric scrapes my cheeks. A sharp pain explodes at the back of my head before everything goes black.

Chapter Three

When I awake, a stabbing pain behind my eye beats in rhythm to the echo of water dripping in the distance. The floor is hard, and the air is cold enough to make me shiver. It takes a moment to remember what happened—I was going after Savryn with his bow when someone stuck a bag over my head and knocked me out.

My vision blurs, and I blink a few times to sharpen my surroundings into clearer focus. I appear to be in a dungeon, behind bars, lying on a thin pallet.

You have got to be fucking kidding me.

My wrists are bound, tied so my palms are carefully flattened together. I hope that's a coincidence and not because someone knows it's the only way to prevent me from accessing my magic, but I suspect luck isn't on my side.

Boot steps shuffle beyond the bars of my tiny cell, and I take a moment to gather myself before I look up, sure I already know who's standing on the other side.

When I do finally lift my head, it's not surprising to find the jackass who broke into my shop standing over me, a smug expression on his ugly face. He crouches down so he's nearly at eye level with me, his elbows braced on his knees and his hands hanging loosely between them.

"Hey darling," he says. "If you'd just come with me when I asked so nicely, none of this would have been necessary."

I say nothing, glaring at him as I struggle against my restraints. The man chuckles as he looks me over, lingering far too long on my breasts before his gaze drags lower, and I never, ever want to be privy to the vile thoughts in his misshapen head.

"If you ask me nicely, I'll help you sit up," he says, making me go still. If this bastard touches me, I'm going to saw off his finger with a blunt knife.

"Fuck you," I snarl.

He laughs again and then stands, pulling a ring of keys from his pocket. "A right feisty bitch. My favorite kind."

I suck in a breath through my nose, willing my anger to settle. I'm not scared. I've been in far worse scrapes than this, and I can handle myself, but I'm going to make this fucker *suffer* before I kill him.

The door squeaks on its hinges as he walks into my

cell, stopping just short of where my cheek presses into the pallet. He bends over and hauls me onto my knees. I want to resist, but he's squeezing my upper arm so tightly that it's making my eyes water where his fingers pinch my skin.

Oh, he will suffer slowly, that's for fucking sure.

"Get up," he says, hauling me to my feet and then shoving me out of the cell. "He doesn't like to be kept waiting."

I want to ask who *he* is, but I already understand that no answer will be forthcoming.

I allow myself to be dragged along, but only because the sooner I can figure out what these assholes want, the sooner I can rip out their hearts, feast on their flesh, and get back to my shop. They'll all have to die, no question about that. If they know what I am, I can't allow for any survivors. I just hope they've kept this secret close so I don't have to embark on the messy task of killing too many people.

The man shoves me up a narrow, winding staircase until we emerge into a dark hallway. I'm dragged through a corridor until we arrive at a door that reveals a nearly empty room, save for a chair placed in the center. I don't bother resisting as he shoves me into the seat and then binds me to it with a rope wrapped around my chest. With my hands bound, I'm forced to sit at an awkward angle, so I can't possibly get comfortable.

Next, he bends down and starts securing my ankles to

the legs, his sweaty, disgusting hand lingering on my bare calf. I react, kicking out, catching him in the nose. He flies back, and I watch with satisfaction as he collides against the hard stone with a cry. Smirking, I watch as he curls into himself, his nose and face bloody and his eyes already swelling.

"You fucking cunt," he snarls when a deep laugh from the door draws both of our attention.

"Percy, is our *guest* giving you some trouble?"

A man, a very tall man with wavy dark hair, leans in the doorway, chuckling at the rat-faced Percy with an amused gleam in his eye.

"Bitch kicked me," he says, his voice thick with blood, as though that's not painfully obvious. *This* is the worst kind of man—not just stupid, but stupid and mean.

"Did you do something to warrant being kicked?" asks the second man, and Percy grunts.

"She's our prisoner," he whines. I roll my eyes, and the newcomer shakes his head.

"She's our *guest*," he says, his tone brooking little patience before his gaze falls on me.

He studies me, and I lift my chin, trying to maintain some semblance of dignity, even if I'm trussed up like a pig. Slowly, he looks me over, his gaze skating from the top of my head down to my feet. There's nothing suggestive about it—just a casual perusal assessing a worthy opponent.

While he takes his sweet time, I study him back.

He's big, that's immediately evident. Muscled and obviously in very good shape. His skin is a deep olive hue, suggesting he spends a lot of time outside, a fact that's further evidenced by the smattering of freckles across the sun-kissed skin of his perfectly angled cheekbones. His dark eyes reflect in the dimness of the room, and he's dressed finely, if simply, in a tunic and leather breeches that mold to his body in a not-unpleasing way.

So he's some rich asshole who sent his goon to knock me out and kidnap me. A trader, maybe? Or worse—maybe a politician. He's a bit too attractive for that, though.

When he's finished his evaluation, he walks to the side of the room and drags a second chair over, placing it in front of me before he sits down, straddling it backwards. I lean away as much as my restraints will allow as he rests his arms on the back and gives me another once-over.

"It's nice to meet you," he says.

"I wish I could say the same."

His answer is a devious smirk that I'm sure wins over everyone he's ever met. Unfortunately for him, I've lived a very long time, and I've encountered his type more times than I can count.

I shift, my shoulders starting to ache from my restraints. "Who the fuck are you, and why am I here?"

He tips his head and peers at me as a searing prickle

works its way over my scalp. "I think the question is, who are *you*?"

I snort and wrinkle my nose. "You stole me. Surely, you already know."

"Hmm."

Percy has now recovered from his kick to the face, cradling his nose with a cloth he's procured as he shoots daggers from his beady little eyes.

"I think you're pretending to be Vespera, crusty village healer and procurer of tonics and herbs for your everyday aches and pains," the better-looking one says.

"That *is* who I am," I say. "And who the hell are you calling crusty?"

I know I'm an adept liar, and he won't read the truth in my words—I've been practicing this for centuries. He makes a tutting noise, and a wave of anger swirls in my chest. Who does this bastard think he is?

"I think you're someone else," he says, and Percy the weasel snickers in the corner like he's enjoying this. I'm not sure which of these two I'll kill first. Maybe I'll flip a coin, or I'll just take care of them both at once. "Calanthe, isn't it?"

I don't react. At least, I try not to. Not only because I've always kind of hated the name my mother gave me but because *that* name is supposed to be dead, buried, and gone. Lost to time and memory when Calanthe met with an unfortunate accident on the Cliffs of Destruction all those years ago. *Calanthe* has been dead for decades.

I furrow my brow in my best imitation of befuddled confusion. I should win awards for these performances.

"Excuse me?"

I don't deny it. I don't repeat the name. I don't ask who Calanthe is because all of those things will give me away. Liars always ask too many questions and give too many details. I pretend like I don't even hear what he said.

Unfortunately, it doesn't seem to work as his face stretches into a knowing smile.

"Come now. Don't play coy with me. I know who and *what* you are."

"I don't know what you're talking about." I tug on my restraints. "You have the wrong person. Now, let me go."

The man lets out a breath as he runs a hand through his thick, dark hair. It will truly be a shame to lose such a pretty face with such an appealing jawline when I gut him and hang him up for the crows.

He laughs with a low and dangerous chuckle before he pushes up from his chair and then drags it away.

"I don't think so," he says. "We're just getting to know one another, and I need your help."

"My *help*?" I bite out. "You've just abducted me and are keeping me against my will. In what world do you think I'm ever going to *help* you?"

"That was unfortunate," he says, and my eyebrow climbs up my forehead. "But you refused Percy's invitation and left him with no choice."

"No choice but to knock me over the head and drag me here?"

He spreads his hands in a gesture of innocence, and I inhale a furious breath.

"If you'll hear me out, you'll understand I have a good reason for all of this."

"I will not *hear you out*. Let. Me. Go."

I sit up straight and pin him with a cold look. He bends down, placing his hands on each of my armrests as I lean back, trying not to notice that he smells rather nice.

"Then I'm going to force you to admit who you are," he says.

"There's nothing to admit."

He stands up. "Very well. Then, I guess you'll be spending some time with us."

"I'll take her back to her cell," Percy says, eyeing me up and down and licking his lips like he's planning to eat me for supper. I guess he hasn't learned his lesson about fucking with me yet. But he will. "I can take care of her."

The mysterious man raises an eyebrow at Percy. "That won't be necessary."

I try not to show my relief at those words.

At that moment, a woman appears in the doorway, almost as if by magic. She's dressed in a long grey gown tied at her neck with silver halter straps, the skirt flowing to the floor, the shape formless and light. She wears a silver circlet with a jewel resting against her forehead, her long red curls cascading down her back and over her creamy white shoulders.

"Your Majesty," she says with a deferential curtsy, her hands clasped. *Majesty.* That address sends a sliver of dread needling up my spine. He's not just some brigand who's abducted me. He's royalty. The memory of that ominous skull carved into the side of a mountain overlooking Twilight's End surfaces, but I stuff it away. It *can't* be him. Granted, it's not like any member of royalty is better than another.

"Please show our guest to her room, Celeste." She straightens from her curtsy and sweeps towards me on light feet before Mystery Man looks back at me. "Your options are to go peacefully with your lady's maid to a room fit for a guest, or I can let Percy take you back downstairs."

He pins me with a dark look, and his meaning is clear. If I choose to behave, he won't release me to that wretched little creature posing as a man. It's not much of a choice, but I suppose it *is* one, and I'm not foolish enough to cause trouble just for the sake of it. I'll play his game for now. I'm not going anywhere until I find out what he knows about me and *how* he knows it.

I tip my chin in understanding, and he bends to sever the ropes binding me to the chair, being painfully careful not to touch me. At least he's one step above that rat Percy, who's snarling at me like it's my fault his master isn't handing me over. I think I've decided that one dies first. No one will mourn this idiot, I'm sure.

The mysterious stranger holds out a hand to me. "May I?" he asks, and I nod, wondering why he's pretending to be so polite. If he thinks he'll trick me into trusting him, he's got the wrong witch. He grips my arm and helps me stand.

"Can you take these off?" I ask, gesturing to the ropes around my wrists.

He smiles, his eyes crinkling at the corners in a way that makes my chest tight. "Perhaps if you'd listen to my request."

My nostrils flare in irritation. Fine. I suppose I expected that.

"Not interested," I reply, and he tips a nod in my direction.

"Follow me, my lady," Celeste says with a curtsy. "Please."

She turns and walks for the door, but I stop just as I'm about to leave the room. "Can I at least know who I'm a *guest* of?"

The man turns to me with an expression that gives away nothing.

"You might have heard of me," he says, the corner of his mouth crooking up. Gods, the arrogance on this one. "Most people know me as the Feral King."

Chapter Four

*F*uck. *Fuck. Fuck.*

No. No. No.

The Feral King. How is this possible? He can't be. That man is a liar. But as I follow Celeste up from the dungeons and through the hallways, it's obvious we're in a massive and opulent castle.

Everything is made of dark stone, hung with dark tapestries, and lined with dark rugs. Flickering black candles held by tall iron candelabras guide our way. A glimpse past a window reveals the ocean outside, just past the cliffs, where I know plenty of bodies have found their bitter ends.

What does the Feral King want from me? The audacity to think I'd do anything for him. It makes a little more sense for him to know who I am—he'd have resources and connections all over the kingdom. That thought quells a flutter of worry, knowing he's not just some random bastard who found me out.

Except, not really, because he's the fucking Feral King.

I've had more than enough of kings to last me lifetimes, especially ones who transform into monsters to terrorize their subjects. I recall the story I heard in the market just last week—the king accosted a group of villagers returning from a nearby town in his beast form, ripping them limb from limb and leaving them to rot. The rumors claimed it was punishment for failing to pay taxes on their farm.

Help him. I'd rather die.

Celeste walks at a measured pace in front of me with her hands clasped while I try not to freak out. No, this is fine. I've been in worse situations than this. I just have to convince him he has the wrong person and be on my merry way—once I discover how he uncovered my identity.

Killing a king without causing a fuss might be a little more complicated, but I'm no stranger to assassinations. I'll just need to be a little more cunning. Poison often works well in these cases. Something that makes it look like an illness while his brain bleeds out. I'll just have to figure out how to acquire the necessary ingredients.

Celeste looks over her shoulder with her eyes wide, and I decide she'll be easy enough to recruit to my cause. A few well-placed threats and a little sinister whispering should do the trick. I give her an imperious look and peer down my nose, ensuring she sees me as a threat. The way her eyes spread even wider before she quickly looks away tells me it works.

It's not her fault that she's been saddled with me—this wicked king probably forces these people to work for him, but she's still an obstacle in my way, and I have no issues taking down innocent bystanders when it suits my personal agenda.

We finally arrive at a door, and she stops before turning the knob and holding it open. I enter the room and take in my surroundings, reluctantly impressed. Though it's a little dark and sinister with its black furniture and black everything, I'll admit the room is lovely, in an ornate way. Even if it is just a fancy prison.

"His Majesty said I'm to attend to whatever you need," she says. "My room is in there. You can call on me at any hour." She points to a door at the far side. "There's this rope," she says, walking over to the bed and tugging it. I hear a distant ringing muffled through the wall. "I'll know if you need me."

I eye the rope dubiously and then twist around to show her my bound hands. "How am I supposed to reach it like this?"

"Oh," Celeste says, a line forming between her brows as she looks from me to the rope and back.

"It's fine," I say. This isn't her doing, so making her

feel bad won't accomplish anything. "I'll be fine. I'll just use my teeth or something."

Her shoulders relax with visible relief. "I'll draw you a bath and call for some food."

Before I can say anything, she scurries through another door to what I presume is the bathroom. That's confirmed when I hear the rush of water from a tap a moment later. Puffing a lock of hair out of my eye, I walk over to the window to look out. My room faces the sea as I expected it would, the window looking over a sheer cliff with nothing but a deadly plunge below. Amusingly, a door leads to a balcony as if there might be something pleasant about standing on a precarious platform dangling over a mouthful of jagged rocks. Some architect must have had a hell of a sense of humor.

It's also possible this room was specifically designed for prisoners, with the balcony serving as a warning. Either way, no one is dragging me out *there*. The rest of the room is decorated in hues of black and silver and grey, the banner colors of the Feral King. A large bed sits against the wall, covered in black drapes and more pillows than could ever be practical, while a small table and an arrangement of soft chairs gather in front of a dark fireplace.

"Your bath is ready, my lady," comes a delicate voice, and I turn around to find Celeste. She waves me over, and I follow her into the spacious room covered in creamy white tiles shot through with veins of silver and black. I wonder why I'm being treated to this grand confinement when he could have easily sequestered me in that dank dungeon.

"I'm to help you out of your clothes," Celeste says reluctantly.

"Actually," I say, "I changed my mind. I don't need a bath."

I step back as my heel hits a step leading up to the tub, stumbling just as Celeste catches me by the elbow. I desperately want a bath after sleeping in the filth of that cell, but she cannot see me without my clothing.

"His Majesty insists," Celeste says. "I'm to..." she swallows hard, her throat bobbing, "...call Percy if you refuse."

That monster. How has he thought of everything?

"Fine," I say with gritted teeth. The only thing that might make this situation worse is that weasel coming anywhere near me, so we may as well get this over with. It would be ridiculous to think I could keep myself covered indefinitely when I don't even have use of my hands.

I have no idea how she plans to manage it, though. That's when she opens a drawer and procures a shiny pair of scissors. Okay then. Seems this king really has thought of everything.

"Is this all right?" she asks, and I can tell she's definitely frightened of me. Good. That's good. That's what I need.

"Sure. I guess the bastard will owe me a new dress." Her eyes widen at the comment, but she proceeds to snip at my garments. After she cuts away the shoulders and the arms, my dress falls to my feet. I'm still naked underneath, given I didn't have the chance to change after Savryn left my shop last night. I wonder if he's realized I'm missing. People will have noticed I didn't open for the day by now, and he's probably looking for his bow. Will anyone care that I'm gone? Will anyone save me? Probably not. Not when they find out where I am. Only a lunatic would try to go against the Feral King. Not even I would save myself in this position.

Her eyes widen at the sight of me, and I grimace at my exposure.

Covered in markings that are the source of my greatest power, black vines and leaves and flowers twist around my arms and legs and torso, along with smaller depictions of animals, objects, buildings, landscapes, and even some names. All the dresses I wear are strategically designed to keep them hidden from prying eyes—high collars and long sleeves—but here, I've been left without a choice.

Her gaze wanders over me, unable to look away. I can't blame her. The tapestry of my skin is my art, and I take pride in its beauty.

"My eyes are up here, sweetheart," I say, and she blinks up, color flushing her cheeks.

"Sorry," she mumbles.

I shake my head and walk over to the tub. Celeste grabs hold of my elbow and helps me maneuver into a sitting position. I'm sort of grateful she's here because otherwise, I would have no doubt slid down onto my ass and probably broken something. Once I'm seated, she asks, "Shall I wash you?"

I nod, trying to hang on to some semblance of my dignity as she soaps me up and suds my hair. Now, my ropes are wet and will probably chafe at my skin. At least I won't have to sleep in the filth of whatever was in that dungeon.

When I'm clean, Celeste helps me out and wraps me in a dry towel. I head into the main room, where a tray of food sits on the table by the windows. I eye a bowl of soup and a few slices of thick white bread, along with some crumbled cheese. As I stare at the food, my stomach rumbles. It's been nearly an entire day since I last ate, and I'm feeling the effects of limited nourishment.

"I have this for you," Celeste says, and I turn around. She's holding up what looks like a nightgown that's been altered to accommodate my current situation. Ties at the shoulders allow her to slip it on from the bottom and then secure it. Goddess, this is humiliating. I'm going to make it hurt so much when I get my hands on the Feral King.

"Thank you," I say, allowing the towel to drop. She's seen it all now, so what's the difference? When I'm suitably covered once again, we both eye the food on the table.

"Would you like me to?" She gestures to the soup and then looks at me with a line between her brows.

"No," I say, shaking my head. Goddess, no, I don't want this girl feeding me. "I can manage from here."

"Are you sure?" she asks.

I realize the situation doesn't look ideal, but I am *not* letting her feed me.

"Positively. Please, go do…whatever it is you do. I'll call if I need you." I gesture to the bell she demonstrated earlier.

"Okay," she answers reluctantly before she backs up a few steps and spins around, her light dress flaring around her before she scurries away, clearly relieved to escape my presence.

When she's gone, I turn back to the food and sit at the table. I'm going to have to just eat this like a dog. Leaning down, I pick up a piece of bread between my lips, trying to chew without dropping it. I work my jaw, clinging to the crust when the end breaks off and lands in the soup, splashing me with crimson drops.

Of course, they served me tomato.

Should I try to lick some up? As I bend over, a lock of my black hair falls forward, nearly landing in the soup. Swiveling my shoulders to fling it back, I consider calling Celeste to tie it up, but I don't want anyone to see me like this.

Tentatively, I bend down and try to lap up the soup, but I'm not a fucking cat, and it dribbles down my chin, bright red spots spreading on my white nightgown like blood. I close my eyes and inhale a deep breath, trying to locate a sliver of patience.

Longingly, I look at the bottle of wine, knowing there's little chance I can work that cork out on my own, which is truly a shame because I've never needed a drink more in my life. I'm also starving, but this isn't working, and suddenly, I'm so spent, I can barely keep my eyes open.

I get up and shuffle over to the bed, rolling my shoulders to ease some of the tension in my joints. Sleeping like this will be wildly uncomfortable, but I reason it's better than the hard cell floor I suffered last night. The bed looks soft, at least.

Not bothering with the covers because that would require too much effort, I sit down, lie on my side, and eventually drift into sleep.

Chapter Five

When I awake again, the sky outside is darkening, the sun setting over the sea. I blink heavily and groan at the ache in my body. Somehow, despite my discomfort, I managed to fall asleep. A soft clink from the other side of the room draws my attention to Celeste, and I heave myself up.

She's cleaned away the remnants of my abandoned supper and is placing an array of brushes and small pots of makeup on the table.

My stomach grumbles loudly, and her gaze darts to my nightgown, where it lingers on the red spots I spilled on myself. She says nothing and looks away. I'm disappointed to see she hasn't brought more food because I think I'm hungry enough to let her feed me after all.

"Celeste," I say, my voice dry as sand. I haven't had

any water in a while, either. "Could I get something else to eat?"

She spins around to face me and clasps her hands together. "Sorry, but you're to have dinner with His Majesty. He wouldn't like it if you've already eaten."

I stifle a groan. Great. Not only will I have to suffer his company, but the bastard won't even let me eat?

I understand his game. He claimed he'd force out my truth, and I can only suppose that should he manage it, he'll blackmail me into supporting whatever power-hungry quest he's intent on accomplishing. These kings are all the same.

"Can I at least get some water then? I haven't had anything to drink since yesterday."

Her eyes dart to the door, as though the king is about to come barging in and scold her for offering me water.

"Please. I promise it's not going to ruin my appetite." I decide being nice, in this case, is a more useful tactic than fear. "I'm really thirsty." I make my voice extra hoarse to drive home the point, which appears to rouse her sympathy.

"Okay, yes. Of course." She hurries to the bathroom, where I hear a clink and the water running. She returns, holding the glass in both hands, and then stops before me. "Should I?"

"Yes," I say, no longer caring about my pride. She nods and then brings the glass to my mouth, tipping it gently. I gulp it back, savoring the cool slide down my throat. I hadn't realized just how thirsty I was until this moment. She uses a cloth to wipe my chin when the glass is empty. I keep it up, pretending this isn't wholly degrading.

"I'm to get you ready," she says with a forced smile. "The king has a wonderful dinner planned for you."

Oh, I'm sure he does.

Celeste directs me to the table and starts to brush my hair and apply my makeup, all while she hums to herself.

"Why are you dressing me up like this?" I ask suspiciously.

She stops and looks at me with a fluffy brush poised mid-air.

"Because I was told to." Her lovely eyebrows draw together.

"No, that's not what I—" I let out a breath. "Never mind."

Why would this girl know what the king has planned?

She finishes her work and then stands back to survey me. Apparently satisfied, she heads towards the closet and flings it open. A moment later, she returns with some garments.

I give her another suspicious look as she holds up a small pair of white underwear. "These first. King's orders," she whispers, and I have no choice but to go along.

I contemplate what the Feral King does to his servants should they disobey him. Do I care what happens to this girl? Not really, but given my circumstances, it's just easier to go along with this.

"Fine." I stand, and she bends down while I step into the holes before she shimmies them up my legs and then my hips.

Next, she holds up a white bandeau, clearly meant to cover my breasts. "This too."

What.

"Take it off then," I say, gesturing to the nightgown with a resigned sigh. She walks over, untying the shoulder ribbons and letting it fall to the floor before she pulls the stretchy fabric up over my hips and then over my breasts. She turns around again and holds up a dress not dissimilar to the nightgown I was wearing, except this time, it's made of sheer white fabric and secures behind my neck.

I gape at the dress, and she gives me an apologetic look before she holds it open for me with a hopeful expression. I sigh again and step into it before she pulls it up and ties the ribbons.

Looking in the mirror, I understand why this has been selected for my attire. Every black marking that covers my skin stands out in stark contrast to the white dress and my brown skin. How did he know? This can't be a coincidence. He's trying to show me he's playing the upper hand while stripping away my defenses. Another prickle of dread works its way up my back.

"If you're ready, I'll take you to his chambers," Celeste says. "Do you like it?"

She looks in the mirror at where I'm staring. She's done a lovely job with my hair and makeup, but I really am not in the mood to care about that right now. The Feral King knows far too much, and I hate how close to the truth he already seems to be.

"Yes, thanks." I give her a smile that feels forced, but what does she want from me?

Then she curtsies. "This way, then."

I follow her through the wide, opulent hallways of the castle, trying to get the lay of my surroundings. Maybe I can just run when an opportunity presents itself. Celeste's long dress sweeps the floor while I survey the high ceilings and arches as we pass underneath. One wouldn't call this place homey—not that I expected it to be.

We walk for what seems like forever before we stop at the tallest doors I've ever seen. They're ridiculous, really. I'm amazed anyone can open them; they must be excruciatingly heavy, but the guard stationed outside seems to do so easily.

I'm ushered down an ostentatious hallway gilded with golden scrollwork until we emerge into a round solarium. The floors are creamy tile, and the windows look out over the sea, where the sun is setting over the horizon, painting the water and sky in warm oranges and pinks. Greenery and plants line the perimeter, and the temperature is at least ten degrees warmer.

A small white table covered with food sits in the center of the room alongside two chairs, and the warm smells make my stomach rumble. The king watches me with his legs crossed and his hands folded over his stomach. He's wearing a crisp white shirt, unbuttoned to show off a smooth expanse of bronze, chiseled chest, along with black pants. Even seated, I can tell they fit him in a way that, under different circumstances, I'd appreciate.

His black boots are polished to a shine, and his hair is slicked back without a single strand out of place. He studies me, his gaze sweeping over me, lingering on the markings that cover my arms, legs, stomach, and chest. They're a map of my life. Depictions of every magic and battle I've ever faced. Allowing him to see me this way feels like offering up an exposed nerve, but I can't let him see me squirm.

His expression was cold, detached, and apathetic the last time we met, but something else lingers in it now. I notice the spread of his pupils as he slowly drags his gaze to mine.

"So glad you could join me," he finally says, his voice low and rough, like he's just on the edge of transforming into his beast.

"I wasn't aware I had a choice."

"You didn't. I was merely being polite. Please, have a seat."

I scoff and walk towards the table. "Don't tell me the Feral King has manners? I thought you were nothing but snarling teeth and hair."

He tenses, and his gaze flashes with a pointed edge.

Then he picks up a decanter of wine, his shoulders relaxing a second later before he lets out a soft chuckle I don't really buy.

"I assure you, my manners are up to the standards of even the most uppity queen."

I clamp down on a smile that threatens to give me away and sit in the chair, doing my best to look dignified. My joints are absolutely screaming, but I don't want him to notice.

"Comfortable?" he asks, his gaze flicking to my shoulders and then back up.

"Very." I pin him with a look. "Why do you ask?"

The corner of his mouth ticks up, and something like amusement dances in his eyes.

"Would you like some wine? Something to eat?"

Fuck yes, I would. My stomach is practically eating itself at this point, and I'd give anything to be blissfully, stupidly drunk right now.

"I suppose that might be nice," I say instead.

He pours sparkling wine into a glass and then holds it out before he makes a sound of mock sympathy.

"Oh, but you can't manage it on your own, can you?"

"You could untie me."

He puts the glass down. "I could, but we both know I won't."

Yes. I figured that.

He then places some items on my plate. Bite-sized morsels of rare meat and melty cheese on top of small rounds of bread, garnished with herbs and flakes of salt and pepper. The smell is incredible, and I can't resist drawing a deep inhale.

I stare at my plate and then look up at the king watching me closely.

"Seems like you're stuck again."

Goddess, what an asshole. My mouth presses together, and I tamp down on my rage, refusing to let him see me ruffled.

"On second thought, I'm not that hungry," I say, scooting back in my seat. There's no way I'm eating like a dog in front of *him*.

But then my stomach grumbles audibly, betraying me completely.

He smiles with a wicked grin. "From what I understand, you've barely eaten since you arrived. You must be absolutely *starving* by now."

Unexpectedly, he leans forward and drags his chair closer by reaching between his legs. When he settles again, his knees almost touch mine, and I sit back, wary about what he has planned.

"I could help you out," he says, his gaze roving me from top to bottom, and I'm confident I'm not mistaking the interest in his eyes. It's not lecherous or off-putting, but something troubling is making it hard for me to look away.

He picks up one of the morsels, and I note how very nice his hands are. Big and strong-looking. The kind of hands that would do a magnificent job gripping my thighs as he fucked me hard against a wall. I blink, willing that image out of my head. Not me. Someone. Someone *else*.

"This is deer," he says, picking it up and sniffing it. "Seared rare and topped with crème fraiche and rosemary. One of my favorites."

"I thought your favorite meal was helpless villagers," I say, and his eyes darken again for a flash. Okay, this is definitely a sore spot. I'll have to remember that. I'm surprised he isn't boasting about it—the way he has everyone trembling under his thumb.

He brings the food closer to my mouth, hovering an inch away. I look down at it, wondering how the hell I found myself here. Two days ago, I was happily riding Savryn in my shop, and now, I'm sitting in a solarium with the Feral King, who's feeding me dinner with his fingers.

He moves it closer until it touches my lip, an amused gleam in his eyes. He's fucking enjoying this. My stomach growls again, and I close my eyes and inhale deeply, willing myself to remain calm.

"Just a bite," he says. "You must be *so* hungry."

It only takes a moment for me to give in. I *am* so hungry, and goddess, it smells so good, and I am only so strong. I open my mouth, and he pops the food in. I bite down so quickly that I nearly take off his fingertips, and it's not entirely an accident. He laughs as I chew and then swallow before he picks up another one.

"Duck and—"

"I really don't care. Just give it to me." He laughs again, the sound like sun-warmed planks of wood.

He does as I ask, popping this one in too, and I chew it and swallow it down. Now I realize just how hungry I was. He feeds me a few more pieces, each more glorious than the last. I moan in appreciation when he pops in a cracker with creamy cheese topped with cranberry jam.

After my plate is clean, he tips his head and then asks, "Dessert?"

Oh, fuck it. I'm here now, and he's already fed me, so what's the harm in allowing him to continue? "Yes."

"I didn't hear the magic word."

A low growl rumbles in my throat as I glare at him.

He chuckles again as he reaches across the table, choosing a bright green macaron and holding it just past my lips.

I look up to meet his dark gaze, and we both go still. Suddenly, my breath feels too shallow, and I'm not sure why. He presses the macaron to my lips, and it's only because I'm no longer starving that it occurs to me how intimate this is. His fingers graze my bottom lip as he pushes the macaron into my mouth, and I shiver, my skin dimpling everywhere. Why does the Feral King have to be so pretty?

His eyes glaze over as he watches me, fixated on my mouth before I swallow and say, "I think I'm good now."

As he leans back in his chair, I notice the color dusting his cheeks.

"Are you all right? You're a bit flushed," I ask.

"I'm fine," he says a little too quickly. "You haven't had any wine yet."

I sigh. "I'd really like to drink it myself." Not only do I want these ropes off, I want to keep him at a distance. This is a distraction I don't need right now.

He arches an eyebrow and crosses one leg over the other as his knee brushes mine. I shiver again, and no, I will not feel anything for this asshole. But goddess, I've always been a sucker for dark hair, firm thighs, and a bit of almost-deserved arrogance.

"I could untie you," he says. "I mean, if you are who you claim you are, then I have nothing to fear by leaving your hands free. However, if you show your true self and prove that you can indeed do what I think you can, then you'll blow your entire cover."

Of course, he's right. If I use my magic to get out of this, then I'll have to kill everyone who's seen me. Maybe everyone in this castle. And that sounds messy. The way he's looking at me tells me he already thought of this and planned to use it against me all along.

"Exactly," I say, pretending he is perfectly logical, and I've already thought of this, too. "So you win either way."

My saccharine smile elicits a derisive snort. He

unfolds his legs, pulls a dagger from his belt, and holds the sharp edge up to the glinting light.

"Exactly," he says.

He stands and leans around me, grabbing hold of my arm. He's so close, and he smells good. Fresh and earthy, mingled with the scent of clean laundry and a hint of something bitter, like whisky or strong coffee. His firm grip on my skin churns a strange rush of energy through my limbs as he slices through the ropes.

My arms pop apart, and I let out a sound that is half groan, half whimper. I rotate my shoulders and roll my neck, trying to loosen some tension.

He's sitting back again, watching me as if waiting for sudden movements. I resist every urge to blast him away with my magic, knowing I'll expose my entire identity, but he looks so smug and, yes, so annoyingly handsome that I wish I could vaporize him to dust.

"Anything you want to do?" he asks, completely at ease. I'll give him this—he's either foolish or brave because if I wasn't pretending to be an ordinary human woman, I could end him without a thought.

I sense he knows that. And that, maybe, it excites him a little.

"Yes. What I want is to go back to my shop with an apology for kidnapping me and a tidy compensation, so I'll never have to work another day in my life."

He tuts as my hands fist against the sheer material of

my dress, fighting the visceral urge to reach down his throat and pull out his entrails.

"Come now. You don't really expect me to buy this simple healer act? Look at you."

He sweeps a hand over me, encompassing the markings all over my skin. Yes, these are sort of hard to explain, I'll give him that.

"Where did these all come from?"

"I have an interest in art," I say. "Of all kinds."

"So you did these?"

I nod. "Some of them. I've had help with others from a master tattooer. They're old. From my youth."

He scrubs his chin, looking at me. "They look quite fresh and dark. You're sure about that?"

"Of course I am. As I said, he's a master."

"Strange hobby for a healing woman."

"When I'm interested in your opinion on how I spend my time, I'll be sure to ask for it," I say.

He grins right before he leans towards me, his knees spreading so my legs are sandwiched between them. "Very well. Hold on to your secrets for now, but I will get them out of you," he says in a low and sinister tone, and for the first time since I've been kidnapped, I'm just a little bit afraid.

Chapter Six

After our dinner, I'm returned to my room, where I enjoy the freedom of using my hands. What a relief it is. I spend a few minutes stretching before the window, watching the churning sea. I consider heading onto the balcony to get a better sense of where my room is in relation to my potential freedom, but when I eye the steep drop, I decide to tackle that task later.

I change out of my demeaning dress after finding something more comfortable to cover my tattoos, and then I sit on a chair and wait. What am I supposed to be doing here, exactly? A pair of guards are stationed outside my door. I could easily deal with them, but I'm not sure how many more I'd have to contend with on my way out. There's a reason I'm being kept in this room, dangling off the side of a cliff.

If anyone sees me using my power, it will take who

knows how many years of hiding to shed my skin and start over yet again. I just don't have the energy.

I sigh, wondering how complications seem to find me no matter how far I run. I've found a certain kind of peace in the life I've built in Twilight's Cove. After I ran from King Malakar, he hunted me for so many years, and there were so many near misses. It was exhausting, and I don't want to do all that again.

Once I discover how the Feral King knows about me and what he wants, I'll look for an escape without my magic. I'm resourceful; I can figure something out. Show me a guard who can resist some feminine wiles when I decide to turn on the charm. I'll have them all eating out of the palm of my hand before long.

The door at the far side of my room opens, and Celeste enters, stopping when she sees my hands in my lap. Her eyes widen with fear as she takes a step back.

"It's fine," I say, holding them up. "The king cut my restraints because he decided I wasn't a danger."

That's not really the truth, but that answer seems to relax her a bit. She's wearing another loose dress, this time in yellow, her red hair piled on top of her head. I wonder what she did to get saddled with my care.

"Can I get you anything?" she asks.

I roll my neck and grab onto my shoulder. "I could really use something to help with this pain. Those ropes did a number on me."

"I have some salve you can use," she says before

she disappears through her door. I presume she must have another exit through her chamber, but I'm sure the king has already considered that, and it's also heavily guarded. As I wait for Celeste to return, I stare at the ocean, watching the waves tumble over each other.

The next two days pass slowly. There's nothing to do in my room, and every book Celeste brings me is another boring textbook that fails to hold my interest. As if I have a need to read about the same history I lived through or the pathetic meanderings of magic that humans call *science*.

"Don't you have any romance novels?" I ask her, tossing aside another useless option. "Ones with lots of sex in them?"

Celeste's cheeks heat, and she looks at the door as if someone might hear her. "I can do that."

Then, she tips her chin and disappears. About half an hour later, she returns with her arms full of books.

"I asked all the girls to give me some of theirs," she says breathlessly as she dumps the entire lot on the bed. "This one is my favorite."

She hands me one.

"*The King and His Captive*," I read, raising an eyebrow as I take it from her.

"It's very..." She waves a hand at her face as if to indicate she's warm, and I can't help but smile. "We've got lots more if you finish with these."

She beams at me expectantly, and I can tell she's thrilled to have been so useful.

"This is perfect," I say, and she squeals with a little hop. She's honestly so sweet. It really would be a shame if I had to kill her.

"I'll leave you to it." Then, she scurries out of the room once again.

Sitting on the bed, I pick up the *King and His Captive*, definitely intrigued, before I scoot back and lean on the headboard.

If nothing, the Feral King knows how to play the role of the proper host, and I'm supplied with all the food and wine I can consume. Now that I'm no longer restrained, I've been taking full advantage of it, so I pour myself a glass and settle back with the book, deciding that maybe this isn't so bad after all. It's almost like a vacation from my life. I could use a little break from the grind of my shop.

Being the only healer in Twilight's Cove—one who's actually effective—can be demanding, as someone always needs a cure or tonic.

I think of the Eben family and hope they're managing. Their little one will be due for a refill of my coughing remedy soon, and it's the only thing that provides the boy with some relief. Old Mister Joss will also need some of his ointment before long. I bite my lip in worry, wondering how much longer this nonsense will keep me here.

But I'm sure the king is already realizing he won't be able to drag my secrets out. Why else have I been sitting in this room doing nothing for so long? Once I trick him into telling me how he knows about my gifts, I'll be back at my shop soon enough.

At that, I sit back and crack open the book, settling in to enjoy an afternoon of reading. Everything will be fine.

Chapter Seven

Obviously, I am a complete fool for trying to convince myself of that.

The very next day, my wish for some "excitement" materializes in the form of a loud thud on my door. I don't bother getting up from my bed, where I spent the night reading *The King and His Captive* from cover to cover. I enjoyed it very, very much.

After a moment, it swings open, and one of the king's guards stands in the doorway.

"You are summoned to the Feral King."

I sigh and scoot to the edge of the bed.

"Very well. Take me then."

"Not like that," the guard says, pointedly not looking at me but at his feet. "He's asked that you dress appropriately."

"What is that supposed to mean?"

The guard's eyes flick up with an unvoiced plea, begging me to understand. I shake my head, and then it occurs to me. The dress that shows off my tattoos. The king still wants me to understand that he's not letting this go.

"Fine," I say. "Give me a moment, then."

I consider calling for Celeste, but I know where she stored the dress, and I can manage on my own. I grab the items and head into the bathroom, where I strip down and don the flimsy garments. I smooth the sheer fabric over my stomach, admiring the pleasing shape of my curves.

You could ask me how many years I've lived, but I'd tell you I stopped counting at least a century ago. Give or take three, maybe four hundred? I don't really know. The point is that I still look like a human woman in her absolute prime. A fact that affords me many advantages in this life and one I use liberally. This king will be no different.

When I'm dressed, I head back into the main room, where the king's soldier waits.

"I'm ready," I say, and he nods before spinning around and heading for the door.

Then, we're on the move through the castle again. I attempt to snatch glimpses of my surroundings, but all I see are stretches of ocean through every window. It's like the king has specifically planned this route, so it's impossible to map out an escape. Highly inconvenient.

We descend into the bowels of the castle, where I'm

denied any sort of view thanks to the complete absence of windows before we arrive at a small iron door. The guard heaves it open, revealing an empty room with a chair in the center.

Well, it doesn't take a genius to figure out what's about to happen.

"Sit," the guard says predictably. I do so, settling into the seat when two more bodies enter the room a moment later. The king and Percy both walk in, and I wrinkle my nose. Percy holds a thick coil of rope in his hand and wastes no time heading towards me, but the king sticks out his arm and blocks him.

"I'll do it," he says, and Percy frowns at the king, who ignores him. The king takes the rope and starts to wind it around my upper arms, binding me to the chair. I wince as it touches my skin. When I look closer, I realize it's not ordinary rope. Fine filaments of copper thread are woven through the rough hemp.

"Copper is... troubling for witches, isn't it?" the king says conversationally, like he doesn't know exactly what he's doing.

"I wouldn't know," I say, trying not to shift as the burn starts to delicately cook my skin.

The king has added just enough that it doesn't cause instant pain but also enough that it will soon become uncomfortable. This deficiency isn't typically much of an issue since copper is easy enough to avoid. Once again, I'm troubled by the depth of his knowledge about my kind. These are secrets we keep closely guarded for reasons just like this.

His answering laugh is low and dark as he picks up my wrist and places it on the armrest. A flare of heat scorches the spot where he touches me. Obviously, it's not the same kind of heat as the copper, but I still do my best to ignore it. I will not be attracted to this asshole, no matter how pretty he is.

He's basically torturing me right now.

If only pain and I didn't have such a complicated relationship.

He straps my wrists to the chair but leaves my hands free so I can use my magic to reveal myself.

"In case you get any ideas about killing the two of us," he says as he moves to my other wrist. "My guards have been instructed to let you rot here in this chair for as long as it takes for you to die, as well. The walls are also warded against magic, so you will be trapped."

None of these 'precautions' would actually stop me, but I look up at him, willing rage into my expression. "I'm not who you want," I say. "Let. Me. Go."

"We'll see about that," he says, circling around to test my restraints.

Percy snickers, his ugly face screwed up into a weaselly smile. What a positively repulsive creature.

"Are you ready?" the king asks, and I look back at him.

"Ready for what?"

He crouches down and pulls something out of his

pocket. More copper. A raw nugget this time and infinitely more potent than the threads currently binding me.

He reaches out and touches the copper very lightly to my ankle bone. The resulting shock ripples through my limbs, like I've just been struck with a tiny bolt of lightning.

"How does that feel?" he asks.

"Fine. Doesn't bother me. You're wasting your time."

I hope I don't sound as breathless as I feel.

"Hmm," he responds as he touches me again, this time halfway up my shin. Fuck. I grit my teeth as another flash of pain spears into my gut. He doesn't give me a chance to recover as he moves it higher, touching the inside of my knee.

I don't react. I can't react.

This is nothing. I'm a normal human woman.

"Doesn't hurt?"

"Not at all," I croak.

It's so very obvious that I'm lying.

He moves higher, touching the inside of my thigh, and I groan because suddenly, another sensation beyond just the pain materializes. A flare in the space between my thighs and a tingling in my nipples. I've always had a bit of a thing for pain, particularly when it's meted out by a handsome man. But this should *not* be turning me on.

After I inhale a deep, cleansing breath, he pulls the copper nugget away. I look down at him, suddenly very aware that he's crouched between my spread thighs. The tiny scrap of fabric covering me is hardly a barrier at all. It would take very little for him to lean over and bury his face into my wet pussy.

Wait. Do I want that?

His eyes have gone dark as his jaw clenches, and I swear to the goddess, he's feeling something, too. Something that's confusing him? Or maybe making him reconsider things.

"Keep going," I whisper, infusing my voice with seduction. "Whatever you're doing isn't working."

He lifts his hand, and I open my legs a little wider, inviting him in, hoping to confuse him a little more. His nostrils flare, and his mouth presses into a straight line as he concentrates very hard, touching the copper in the same spot. My reaction has a mind of its own as my head tips back, and I let out a sound that's part moan and part gasp.

He drags it higher ever so slowly, bit by agonizing bit. The tip of his thumb brushes my sensitive inner thigh as my entire body reacts. He runs a hand over his face, and his precarious proximity to where I'm wet and aching can't possibly be the outcome he had in mind.

He continues dragging the nugget higher until he reaches a spot just inches from the apex of my thighs. His knuckle brushes the soaking-wet fabric of my underwear, and my pussy tightens with a throb. I can't tell if he did that on purpose or by accident, but his pupils blow out, suggesting he's aware.

Instead of retreating, I open my legs even wider and then pin him with a look, daring him to proceed.

"That's enough," he says sharply, backing up so abruptly that he nearly stumbles. His cheeks are flushed, his eyes a little wild.

"Problem?" I ask, blinking up at him innocently.

His dazed expression turns thunderous, and it's obvious he's pissed off that his plan didn't work.

"Take her back to her room," he says to Percy, and I blink. I'd completely forgotten he was here.

The king then storms out, slamming the door behind him, avoiding my gaze. I smirk at his back and award myself a point in whatever game we're currently playing.

Percy snickers, and my attention returns to him.

In the heat of the moment, I'd momentarily forgotten about the ropes burning my skin. Percy unties me, revealing some redness, but it's not the worst. Marks dot the inside of my leg, too, but they'll heal well enough soon. Witches tend to recover faster than humans.

Percy circles his sweaty hand around my arm, and I yank it away. "Don't touch me."

His face darkens. "Don't speak that way to me, witch." He raises his hand and is about to strike it across my face when someone calls out.

"Halt," says one of the king's guards. "She isn't to be touched." His tone suggests Percy already knows that and definitely should know better. What is this? The king just spent his morning torturing me, but no one is allowed to hit me? If this weren't all so annoying, I might start laughing at the absurdity of my predicament.

"Fine," Percy snarls at the guard and then at me. "Let's go."

We march through the castle with Percy in front and the guard bringing up the rear until I'm delivered to my room. I slam the door gratefully and lean against it as I ponder my surroundings. The Feral King will try again with a different tactic next time. Something that is decidedly less pleasant.

My pussy is still aching, though, and I really need to do something about it. Between the king's big body nestled between my thighs and the book I read last night, I'm definitely more than a little wound up.

I march over to the window and shuck off my white underwear before opening the door to my balcony. I don't dare step out, but I savor the breeze that blows up under my dress, hoping to cool myself off. Honestly, though, this is making me even hornier. So, I pull up a chair and plop down while dragging a second one over to prop up my leg. Then, I spread myself open and allow the breeze to caress my fevered skin before I slide a finger through the slick wetness.

Slowly, I stroke my clit, feeling my stomach tighten. I imagine the king on his knees, looking up at me through dark lashes as he touches me with copper. The smokiness in his voice and his intense eyes. The hard muscles in his shoulders that I want to sink my teeth or my nails into. I bet his ass would feel magnificent cupped in my hands as he fucked me hard into the mattress. Or against a wall. Or literally anywhere.

Should I be having these thoughts about my captor? Probably not, but I never claimed my relationships were healthy.

I'm panting now, slickness coating the inside of my thighs as I dip a finger inside me and use my cum to circle my clit, adding more pressure. I'm so close, but I hang on, wanting to hold on to the sensation just a little longer. With another sweep of my finger, I start making harder circles, feeling the tension build until I blow apart with a cry. I continue touching myself, drawing out the aftershocks until I finally feel like I can think again.

When I've caught my breath, I decide to take a long, hot bath as I await my next punishment.

Chapter Eight

Over the next few weeks, my torments are decidedly less interesting. Sometimes, I'm left to stew in my room for a few days, and sometimes, they come back-to-back with no break in between. There is a seventy-two-hour period where they won't let me sleep. They sit me in that fucking chair and tie me with those ropes before leaving me there for hours, forcing me to remain awake. The king keeps his distance the entire time, but he's ready to snap his fingers in my face anytime I drift off.

"Calanthe," he says, sometime in the wee hours of twilight, his voice practically a growl. "If you'd just agree to hel—"

"I'm not helping you," I snap before he can finish. "And that is *not* my name."

Finally, they give up on that, and when the king unties

me, we both stare at the reddened welts on my arms and my wrists before we exchange a look loaded with questions.

No human woman would react to the copper ropes this way. My secret dances so close to the surface that it's hardly even a secret anymore. But now, this has become a battle of wills. If he thinks he'll break me, he's sadly mistaken. How long will he carry on before he finally gives up on this?

I won't give him what he wants. If he kills me in his wayward quest, then so be it. I'd rather become food for the vultures than bind myself to the will of another power-hungry king.

On another occasion, they give me some kind of drug intended to make me hallucinate all my nightmares, but I'm a witch, and things like that don't work on me the way they do on mortals. So, I put on a show, screaming and wailing and grabbing my hair until I pretend to pass out from fear. It took a colossal effort to keep my surprise in check when the king scooped me up and carried me back to my room, where he held me for several long seconds before gently laying me on the bed. He'd remained in the room, and I swore I could feel the weight of his stare. I resisted the urge to peek until he sighed and walked away.

Another time, they tie me to a giant block and force me to drag it through the castle hallways until I collapse. My body gives out because physical endurance is not high on my list of skills or interests. At least not *this* sort of physical endurance. I wake up in my bed and can't move for two days due to the soreness in my muscles and joints.

Through it all, Celeste watches over me with all the care of a fussy mother hen. Fear and worry shadow her emerald eyes as she tends to my burns. She sits by my side for three entire days as I recover from sleep deprivation.

Through it all, the king grows more and more frustrated. I can see it in how his shoulders wind tighter and the increasingly heated force of his glare.

These torments are child's play, though, and he'll have to try a lot harder if he thinks I'm giving up my secrets. Maybe the Feral King isn't quite as dangerous as he would have everyone believe because he could do much worse than this. I've considered asking him to try the copper again because a part of me took sadistic pleasure in the exchange.

I won't lie and say that I haven't touched myself a few more times, imagining his strong body crushed against mine. All the novels Celeste brings to fill my empty days do nothing to tamp down my colorful fantasies.

It's now been two days since my last round of torture—and it might have been the worst of the lot. They put me in a room with *Marigold*, the single most annoying human on this plane. She talks my ear off for eight solid hours about her bunions, the crick in her neck, and the fact that her husband hasn't fucked her in about two decades. How could he? He'd never get a word in edgewise.

It's the closest I come to breaking since my arrival. In my head, I devise a slew of punishments, each more violent than the last. They all involve removing her tongue.

When they finally relieve me, I don't wait to see who's at the door. I just bolt and run for my room, having learned more of my way around. When I try to sleep, all I hear are her nasally words running through my head, like she's bored a hole into my skull before stuffing her voice inside, ensuring it will follow me for all of eternity. I shudder at the very thought.

It's mid-afternoon when Celeste and I are playing cards at the small table by my window when a knock comes at the door. The king enters as it swings open, and I blink in surprise. He's never come to my room in all my weeks here, save the time he carried me when I was pretending to be unconscious.

Behind him marches rat-faced Percy with a snivelly smile on his face. What's that asshole grinning about? Celeste and I exchange a look.

"Can we help you?" I ask as the king stops in the middle of the room, looking around. Everyone waits in bemused silence as he surveys his surroundings.

When he notices the table piled high with smutty books courtesy of Celeste, he approaches and picks up the

King and his Captive. His gaze finds me as he arches an eyebrow.

"Good book?" he asks with a smug tip of his mouth.

I shrug. "It's okay. The king's cock is disappointingly tiny, and he has no idea how to use it."

Celeste claps a hand over her mouth to contain her gasp as the king's eyes darken, but I can't put a name to the emotion I'm seeing.

Anger? Lust? Or perhaps a challenge?

He returns the book to its pile and then gestures casually to Percy, his gaze pinned to mine. "Get her."

Rolling my eyes, I prepare myself for the inevitable, wondering what they have in store for me today, but Percy doesn't reach for me. Instead, he grabs Celeste by the arm and drags her up from her chair.

"Come on, lovely," he sneers as he flings open the balcony door and shoves her outside.

I'm on my feet in an instant. "What's going on?"

The king approaches, towering over me.

"We're taking things up a notch, Calanthe."

To my horror, Percy is now lifting Celeste up on the railing as she screams and flails against his tight hold.

"What are you doing!" I cry out.

"Since nothing seems to *move* you, perhaps you'll react differently when someone else's life is at stake."

Goddess. I didn't anticipate this. But I can't let him realize this might work. Though I previously harbored no reservations about killing her, this sweet little girl has grown on me in the past few weeks. She's shared her life and her hopes and her dreams. The boy back at home she hopes to marry someday, and the money she sends to her family that she earns working for the king. She's a nice girl who doesn't deserve this.

The king grabs me and drags me out onto the balcony, too. If he knew how terrified I was of heights, he could have already found a way to break me. Instead of threatening to shove *me* off this cliff, they're threatening poor Celeste.

"Go ahead," I say, summoning every ounce of self-control I can muster. "You think I care what happens to my jailer?"

Percy sneers in our direction and then tips Celeste forward so she's dangling over the edge. She screams, the sound piercing as her arms windmill against nothing but air. The wind blows her hair away from her face, and I glimpse the terror in her expression.

My hands curl at my sides, my magic practically burning my fingertips. I could do something about this, but I can't reveal what I am. If the king has proof of my abilities, he'll blackmail me into helping with whatever devious scheme he's orchestrating.

Percy shoves Celeste. Just a little. Just enough that her rear slips off the railing, and she drops. My heart wedges in my throat as I lean over to find Percy gripping her by the wrists as she kicks and flails and screams and *screams*.

When I glance down, the entire world spins as my

stomach lurches. I close my eyes, trying to steady my breathing, before I turn around and face the king.

"Go ahead," I say, hoping to the goddesss I'm calling his bluff. I know he's the Feral King, but would he really kill this innocent girl in cold blood? I remind myself of the stories and that he's notorious for the way he's ripped through entire villages, leaving no one and nothing alive. Why would he care about one girl?

But I swear I've witnessed something softer in him.

Something that convinces me he's more man than beast. I hope I'm right.

"Pull her up," the king says to Percy, and I breathe out a sigh of relief. "Stand her on top."

"What? No," I say as Percy forces Celeste to stand on the railing, just wide enough for her feet. She's still screaming, the sound so wild with abandon that I wince.

"I'm going to count to three," the king says, turning to me. "And then Percy is going to shove her off."

"You're a fucking monster!" I cry.

"You said you didn't care."

"I don't. That doesn't mean you aren't a monster!"

"One," he says, looking at Percy and then at me as he steps closer. I retreat, my back hitting the railing. *Don't look down.* Instead, I watch Celeste, tears streaming down her cheeks. She's crying so hard, I'm amazed she hasn't already fallen off.

"Two," the king says, his voice low and dark, his gaze never wavering. If he feels any remorse or contrition regarding his actions, he's hiding it very well. "You can save her Calanthe."

My jaw hardens, and I huff out an angry breath. This asshole will not break me.

"Thr—"

"No!" I shout and then react without thinking as several things happen at once.

As I touch a mark on my neck and then one on my left elbow, Percy reels in to give Celeste a hearty shove as I send out two ribbons of magic. One hits Percy and sends him crashing into the far railing while the other snags around Celeste's waist, tugging her to safety before she collapses in a heap. I rush to her, falling to my knees and wrapping her in my arms as she sobs against my shoulder.

The king's shadow falls over us, and I look up, trying to incinerate him with the heat of my glare.

But my anger appears to have no effect. If anything, he actually seems a bit more relaxed, his shoulders down and his hands hanging loose at his sides.

Then, he crouches to eye level and says, "*Finally*, we're getting somewhere."

Chapter Nine

"You are a vile, horrid piece of filth!" I hiss as Celeste continues to sob against me. She's trembling like an autumn leaf, about to crumble off the tree.

"I wouldn't have let her fall," he says, and I narrow my eyes, not believing a word. It doesn't matter. That was close enough, and he's a brute for treating her this way. I drag her to her feet and escort her back to the safety of my room.

I sit her down at the foot of the bed and pour her the strongest glass of liquor I can find before I press it into her hands. "Drink it all," I order, and she stares at it only for a second before she tips the entire contents back. I pour her another, pointedly ignoring the king.

"This one, too," I say, and Celeste drains the glass as

the color slowly returns to her cheeks. "That's better. Lie down."

After I fluff up the pillow, she does as I say, lying on her side with her hands under her head, her body curled up like a frightened child before I whirl on the king.

"You had no right to do that to her and no right to do any of this to me. You came to my home and stole me from my life, bringing me here to torment me. Give me one good reason I shouldn't kill you right now! You know my secret, so I have no reason to hold back."

He holds up his hands in a gesture of surrender. "Hear me out. There is a reason I did all of this, and I need you to listen."

"Why should I? I don't owe you a damn thing."

"You're right. You don't. Please, I beg you. Hear what I have to say, and if you decide my cause isn't worthy of your help, then I'll let you go with enough gold to keep you comfortable for the rest of your days."

I make a sound of derision and fold my arms, ready to lay down my terms. "Understand this, Feral King—you are no longer keeping me against my will. If I remain in this castle for another moment, it's of my own choosing. You forced me to reveal my power, so fine, well done. But you are at my mercy now and can't even begin to comprehend the ways I could make you suffer."

I gesture to my bare arms, where the black markings of my past are etched into my skin. "These are more powerful than your little mortal brain could possibly fathom, and no one makes me do anything against my will and lives to tell the story for long."

He stares at me for a heartbeat before he dips his chin.

"Understood." Then, he looks up with a dent between his brows. "Will you *please* hear me out then?"

I look over my shoulder at Celeste, who's watching us with wide eyes, still hugging herself on the bed.

"On the condition that once I leave this castle, you will release Celeste from your service and send her on her way with enough riches to ensure that not only can she and her entire family live in extravagance for the rest of her life but so will her children and their children, and their children's children."

"Done," he says without hesitation, and I hear Celeste let out a small gasp. *There.* My good deed is done for the day. Well, it's almost a good deed. She must remain here for the duration of my tenure because I don't want some other annoying maid taking up her position. Goddess, when did I get so soft?

"Fine. I'll hear you out," I say.

"Join me for dinner," he replies, pressing a hand to his chest, suddenly the picture of gentlemanly formality. "I'd prefer to be alone."

"You feel brave, do you, Feral King? Alone with me?" I ask, and his mouth ticks up in a smile.

Why isn't he more afraid of me? He should be. Either

he's a fool, or he's hiding something. At any rate, I can't deny I'm intrigued to hear what's so damn important.

"I also want to know *how* you know who I am," I say. The only reason I'm still here is to puzzle out this mystery so I understand who else I need to deal with.

"That, too, I'll explain," he says.

"Very well," I answer. "I'll join you for dinner."

"Perfect," he says. "Give me two hours, and I'll send for you."

"You'll remove the guards from my door. I am no longer your prisoner. I shall come and go as I please from this room."

He hesitates, wanting to object, but he has no hand left to play. I raise an eyebrow, reminding him of that, and he concedes. "Of course. You have the run of the castle, as would any guest. I'll even assign you one of my personal guards—not to watch over you, but to attend to anything you need."

I can't decide if the offer is genuine or just a smoke screen, but I can handle one guard.

"Good. Now, what are you going to do about him? He's fouling up this entire room with his presence." I gesture towards the window where Percy lies knocked out on the balcony. The king grimaces and runs a hand down his face.

"Do you think you killed him?" he asks. "You would really have done me a favor."

"Excuse me?" I ask with an incredulous laugh.

He gives me a sidelong glance. "Look, he's my cousin, and I'm forced to keep him around. I can't kill him myself because then my mother would kill *me*."

I blink several times, staring at him before I burst out laughing. The Feral King is afraid of his mother. The Feral King *has* a mother? Of course, he does. He's a human man—he must. The expression on his face makes him look like a naughty little boy who's terrified of her wrath.

Bending over, I hold my stomach as I laugh. This might be the funniest thing I've ever heard.

By now, his face has gone deliciously red, and really, it's rather adorable.

"Okay, okay," he says. "You can stop."

I wheeze as I wipe a tear from my eye. "I'm really not sure I can."

That's when his serious frown cracks, and he delivers a wide smile before he shakes his head and rubs his face again. He walks onto the balcony and toes Percy's foot with his boot. Percy groans and rolls over, and the king rolls his eyes, which is strangely endearing.

He crosses my room and opens the door, speaking with the guards. They follow him back outside, each grabbing one end of Percy before heaving him through my chamber and out the door. When they're gone, the king turns to me again and bows.

"I'll see you in two hours, then?"

"Yes, I'll be waiting."

"Thank you," he says, and there's so much sincerity in the sound that I'm almost glad that I agreed to this. His gaze finds mine as his eyes sweep over me, lingering on my mouth before they flick back up.

Then he spins on his heel and leaves.

Chapter Ten

Once the king is gone, I approach Celeste. She's still sniffling, but at least she's stopped shaking.

"Thank you," she says, her voice wobbly. "You saved me."

"Don't mention it," I say, waving a hand as I settle onto the bed. She stares at me, her eyes roaming over my tattoos, and now she's another person who knows I'm more than I've been pretending to be. "Seriously. Don't mention what you saw to anyone."

"Are you a witch?" she whispers.

"Something like that," I say. "But if you want to thank me for what I did, don't tell anyone."

She nods with her eyes wide. "Of course. I would never tell."

I'm sure she means that, but this slip of a girl would

shatter under the merest hint of torture, so it'll have to be the best I can hope for. Maybe if I can acquire some supplies, I can convince her to succumb to a memory tattoo so she forgets this entire thing. It would also relieve any lingering trauma from that unpleasant incident. I'd be doing her a favor, really.

"So, I guess I'm having dinner with the king," I say. "Can you help me get ready? I want to...surprise him."

Celeste sits up, wiping the last remaining tears from her eyes. "What do you mean?"

"Help me look...irresistible," I say, and she pauses for a beat before cracking into a grin.

"Oh, I can do that."

She scoots off the bed and scurries for the bathroom before I hear the clink of the cosmetics and hair products she's so fond of using. Over the next hour, I bathe, and she does my hair and makeup. I look like a goddess when she's done. Something about her skill enhances my features in just the right way. Maybe I should keep her with me instead of insisting the king send her on her merry way when I leave.

To really drive home the effect, I opt for one of the sheer dresses the king provided. It's obvious he holds a measure of attraction towards me despite his reservations, and I plan to use that to my advantage. So the more skin, the better. He's going to regret the day he made me wear these things. He thought he could strip my defenses and my dignity by making me stroll through the castle wearing practically nothing, but I'll teach him a lesson.

I slide on the thin white underwear and the bandeau before Celeste helps tie on the translucent fabric. My arms are bare, and the neckline sinks to my navel, exposing the swell of my breasts and the tattoos covering them, along with those on my stomach. The high slit in the front shows off my entire left leg, and I finally release the magic concealing the tattoos on my hands, feet, and throat. Thank goodness for that. It's really such a bother to keep them hidden.

As I'm adjusting the neckline, a knock comes at my door. Celeste moves to open it, but I hold up a hand and stride over, savoring the sensation of answering it for myself.

A guard stands on the other side, his eyes spreading wide, then dropping immediately to his feet.

"I'm Theron, at your service," he mumbles. "Are you ready to go, my lady?"

"Yes, please lead the way."

Theron leads me through the castle to the same solarium where the king and I first had dinner. The sun is just starting to set over the water, and it's easy to see why he favors this spot. It's the one room that feels warmer and homier than the rest, belying the dark, gloomy castle that perches on the skull-carved mountain towering over the valley.

Theron weaves a path through the lush greenery and then steps aside.

"Your Majesty," he says with a tight bow.

The king stands by the window, looking out before he turns around to face me.

I step forward and offer a curtsey. It's a little impertinent, but I don't really care.

The king goes entirely still as his gaze peruses me slowly, lingering on the swell of my cleavage and the planes of my stomach and pausing where my thighs meet, pulling a tug from deep inside my core. He continues his perusal down my legs and to my feet before he looks up. There is no mistaking the polished lust in his eyes. *Perfect.* Celeste's careful attention achieved exactly what I was going for.

"My king," I say softly, pretending I'm a docile little creature, but he raises an eyebrow, and I hate that he seems to see right through me.

"It's so nice of you to come, Calanthe," he says, again using the name that reminds me of so many things I'd rather forget.

"Please. I'd really prefer to be called Vespera. That name no longer belongs to me."

He nods. "Of course. I apologize."

Theron has already quietly left the solarium, and the king approaches. He takes my hand and presses his warm lips against the back, sending an inappropriate ripple straight to my toes.

It's then I decide that whatever it is he wants from me, I want something from him, too.

Before I laugh in his face about whatever he's about to beg for, I'll make sure to seduce him thoroughly. He's ridiculously handsome, and adding the Feral King to my list of conquests will be a nice little notch in my bedpost.

"So, you know my real name," I say as he leads me towards the table once again laden with a variety of delicacies, each more decadent than the last. "Do I get to know yours? Surely, your sweet mother, whom you hold in such high regard, didn't name you Feral King out of the womb?"

He pulls out my chair, and I settle in it, being sure to let my skirt fall open to expose as much of my legs as possible when I cross them. As he sits down in his chair, I notice his gaze drop before he looks up. He's as buttoned up as usual, wearing a fitted black coat with two rows of golden buttons and black pants that show off his strong thighs. His hair is as neat as ever, and I resist the urge to lean over and muss it up. My chance will come, preferably when his face is buried between my thighs.

He gives me a sly smile as he pours me a glass of wine.

"No, she did not. My real name is Ferran," he says, giving me a look that borders on sheepish.

"Ferran the Feral King?" I ask, and he rubs a hand down his face.

"Yeah. Don't laugh."

"I'm not," I say, taking a sip of my wine to conceal my smile. "It's very nice."

He snorts as he lifts his wine to his lips. "Are you hungry?" he asks after a moment while I survey our meal.

"You're not planning to feed me this time?" I ask, pretending to pout.

"I can if you want." He leans forward, the suggestive glint in his eyes obvious.

I scoot my chair in closer and place a hand on his bicep, giving a firm squeeze to his arm before I drag my fingers down his forearm. "Perhaps after you tell me why I agreed to this dinner?"

"Right. Of course." He looks at the table and spins the stem of his glass, taking a moment to collect himself. "You've heard the…stories about me, I assume?"

I tip my chin. "Of course. I must admit, you aren't quite what I expected."

He pins me with a dark look. "Surely, you should know better than to believe every rumor you hear."

"Fair enough," I concede. "I assume the truth then has something to do with all of this?" I sweep out a hand to encompass all that's happened over the past few weeks.

"It does," he says. "The stories are true. I did all those things. I…killed all those people."

"But?" I ask, tipping my head. Plenty of skeletons live in my closet, and I'm not one to judge.

"The parts about me turning into a beast are true too," he says, and that surprises me a little. I've always wondered if the stories were exaggerated to make him seem more fearsome.

"I was cursed...well, my father was cursed when I was a boy, and that curse passed on to me."

"What did he do?"

"He stole a relic from a powerful mage and tried to use its magic to summon power from the Shadow Realm."

I roll my eyes. "Typical. You kings are all the same, aren't you?"

Ferran says nothing, his nostrils flaring on a deep breath.

"So, let me guess—you want me to find a way to break the curse? Perhaps true love's kiss? How very original."

"No. Maybe. That depends," he says.

That answer also surprises me. "On what?"

He sighs. "When my father used the relic, he accidentally tore a rip in the fabric between our world and the Shadow Realm. The mage refused to close it, citing it as another consequence of his crime. Then, he disappeared with the only thing that would fix it, leaving my father to deal with the aftermath. Ever since, we've been plagued with the demons who slip through.

"Ironically, the ability to shift into his beast form allowed my father to protect this kingdom, and when he died, that responsibility also passed to me. While they vilify my beast, they don't understand that I'm the only thing keeping the Shadow Demons from ravaging the forest and the villages surrounding us. Almost every night, I hunt down and kill as many as I can. But they keep multiplying, and it's never enough."

Now that he mentions it, I suppose it's odd that the demons don't wreak as much chaos as one might expect, but I'd also never considered the matter much further. While humans might live in fear of their presence, very few things in this life scare me.

"Okay," I say. "What do you want from me, then?"

"My first question is: could you close the rip?" he asks. There's so much hope in the question that I feel a measure of remorse for my answer.

"No," I say, shaking my head. "If he used an enchanted object, then you'd need it to undo its effects."

Ferran sighs, his shoulders slumping. "I had a feeling you'd say that."

"Sorry," I say, sort of meaning it.

"In that case, I don't want to break the curse. What I want is to control it. I hurt those people because sometimes the beast takes over, and I can't stop it. It's wild and untamed and absolutely remorseless."

The anguish on his face is clear.

"If you can't close the rip, can you help me with this?"

"How did you find me?" I ask.

"I've been searching for an answer for a very long time. I've had scholars, academics, and every possible resource at my disposal, working around the clock for years. One day, someone came across a story about a witch with the power to use magical tattoos to aid in bodily transformations. I read an account of how she helped a powerful king transform himself into a monster and become so strong that he annihilated all his enemies with only a small army at his back."

I grip my glass tightly as he recounts the tale I know far too well.

"And in that story, I found a glimmer of hope. If she could create a transformation such as that, then perhaps she could control one, too. But the witch died, or so the books claimed, and that hope quickly died alongside her. So, I tasked my scholars to seek another witch like her, but it turned out to be a rare gift, and apparently, no one since had been bestowed with such a talent.

"I was about to give up until, by the strangest of coincidences, one of my scholars who lives in Twilight's Cove has a son who has trouble with his lungs. And so, he went to see the healer woman, who frequently paid them house calls to check on the child.

"One night, after a particularly bad fit, the child's parents were so exhausted that she offered to rock him to sleep so they could catch some rest. She held the child for the entire night, and when the father woke up the next morning, he found them both asleep in a chair. At some point, the healer woman must have undone the high collar on her dress to get more comfortable, and there he saw an array of black markings covering her collarbone."

Ferran pins me with a serious look, and I sip my glass, trying to settle the pounding in my heart. I was careless.

Though I always keep the markings hidden, I also assumed a simple villager who might see them would never think twice about it.

"And then what?" I ask, my voice soft.

"And after all the years he'd spent looking for a tattooed witch, something twigged in his brain. He started to ask around and found someone she was close to. A hunter, I believe? He questioned the hunter, who let it slip that the village healer helped him when he went into the woods. How she could protect him from the demons when he went in search of game to sell at the market."

I swallow a knot of tension in my throat.

Fucking Savryn.

"The scholar told me the hunter was quite drunk at the time, and it didn't seem like his intentions were sinister. He just isn't..."

"All that bright," I say, finishing his sentence. No, I don't think Savryn would have ever betrayed me on purpose, but that was the risk I took when I went for stupid but pretty.

Ferran smirks at that. "A good friend of yours?" he asks, his eyes darkening.

"Something like that," I offer. It's really none of his business.

We both fall silent for a few seconds.

"Why have you been hiding?" he asks me then, and I shake my head.

"I don't want to talk about it."

He nods, letting the matter slide. "So, will you help me?"

"What exactly were your intentions in revealing my magic?"

"You were right—I did hope to blackmail you. You were keeping your abilities a secret for a reason, but I can now see how misguided a plan that was. Why *did* you remain after I freed your hands?"

"Because I had to discover how you knew my secrets. Once I did, I had every intention of breaking out of here, and you wouldn't have been able to stop me."

"I understand that now," he says. "What do you think?"

I consider his question for a moment. "Your cause is noble," I finally say. "Moreso than I would have guessed."

"Is that a yes? I apologize for everything that happened, but I'm desperate. The beast grows wilder every time I change. I'm so close to slipping every single time. A few weeks ago—" he breaks off. "Well, I lost control, and you probably heard about it."

"I did," I say, remembering the mourning villagers in the town square after their friends had been slaughtered on the road. Their sorrow and fear as they all looked upon that stone castle with its skull carved into the mountain, wondering if they would be next.

"Why not tell them? Give them the truth?"

"You really think they'd accept me? All they'll see is

the wild animal that killed their loved ones despite my best intentions. And how can I blame them? They have no reason to believe that I didn't do those things on purpose. It doesn't matter anyway. Their family and their friends are gone, and even if they knew, it wouldn't stop my beast from seeing them as prey. Whether I wanted to hurt them or not is irrelevant. I maintain this persona and hope it's enough to keep them out of the forest and away from the castle, and for the most part, it works."

I nod, conceding he's probably right about all of that.

"I'll need some supplies," I say. "Needles and ink. Herbs and dye."

"Write me a list of everything, and I'll have it here tomorrow," he says. "Along with my gratitude, you'll also have anything else you want that's in my power to give. Gold, jewels, perhaps a nice little cottage in the countryside where you can live in peace forever? Anything."

I nod. "I'll consider that."

"So is that a yes?"

I take another sip of my wine slowly.

"Yes, Ferran the Feral King," I finally say. "I'll help you."

Chapter Eleven

After I agree, we move on to other topics as we eat and drink our dinner. Ferran is surprisingly easy to talk to. He tells me the stories of his youth—the good parts—and even opens up about his father's passing and the curse handed on to him. He'd grown up knowing this was his burden and vowed to protect his people since he was a small child. He shares memories of his mother, who lives in the countryside, where he visits whenever possible.

After a few hours, the wine flows easily, and my cheeks have warmed. The king becomes more and more handsome the longer I'm in his presence, and part of me is glad I'm not leaving just yet. I'm not done with him.

"Tell me," I say finally. "When you were 'torturing me,' seemingly to the best of your ability, did you really think any of that would work?"

He gives me a sheepish grin that makes a dimple pop on his cheek. My goodness, that's appealing.

"I was hoping it would?"

"But?"

"But I really didn't want to hurt you."

I smirk and sip my wine. "Well, isn't that sweet. Just mild torture, then?"

He shrugs. I really should be angrier with him, but I can't seem to muster it.

"Would you have let Celeste fall off the balcony?"

"Absolutely not," he says. "But you two seemed to have bonded, and it was a last-ditch effort to force you into cracking before resorting to more drastic measures."

"Well, aren't you a study in contrasts?" I quip.

He's watching me intently like he has been the entire night. I put down my glass as I stand, and he sits back when I straddle his lap.

Then, he goes very still.

"Is this okay?" I ask, tipping my head, and he nods.

"Yes," he croaks out. "Definitely okay."

"When you were using the copper on my skin, you suddenly got very angry. What was that about?"

He licks his lips, and I watch how his tongue moves, hoping he knows how to use it.

"That was a mistake," he says, his voice thick.

"Oh? Why is that?"

"You…I'm not sure how to say this. You didn't seem to mind it."

I laugh softly. "How very astute of you."

"I thought it hurt. It seemed to hurt, but..."

"Oh, it hurt," I say, touching his face and softly running my fingers down his cheek and along the line of his jaw. He shivers, and the sensation sends gooseflesh across my skin as my nipples peak. I lean forward and press my nose to his throat as I inhale. Gods, he smells good. Like fresh grass and leather and other manly things. "But sometimes, when it's the right kind of pain, offered by the right person, it also feels good."

He blinks and then swallows hard. "And that felt good?"

"It did. It can be intoxicating when pain and pleasure exist as one."

He nods slowly. "I think I understand."

"Do you?"

I shift my hips and smirk as the thick, hardening evidence of his cock presses against my pussy. I knew he wanted me. I roll my hips, grinding myself into him as his hands dig into my flesh. They're so big and strong, exactly like I imagined.

I lean forward again and suck gently on the curve of his neck as I roll them again, my core tightening. I'm already soaked through my underwear. Gods, I could get off just from doing this. What is it about this king that makes me so needy? He lets out a soft moan and then shifts as he pulls me down harder against him.

Now, I can't wait to get him into my tattoo chair and teach him so many things.

As I roll my hips again, I decide there's far too much clothing between us. I reach down and flick open the button of his pants before he grabs my wrist.

"No," he says, a pained edge to his voice. "I'm sorry. I can't do this."

Then, he stands, lifting me like I weigh nothing before he sets me on my feet and deliberately steps around me.

"Theron!" he calls into the solarium, and my guard materializes through the foliage.

"Please take our guest back to her room," Ferran says. He's clearly been shaken, the color high on his cheeks. Then, he turns to me. "Please write down the list of everything you need, and I'll have it delivered immediately. Thank you."

"Of course," I say as I pass, never taking my eyes off him. He follows me with his gaze, the hunger impossible to ignore.

I don't let any of this bother me. He's unnerved and a little frightened because he thinks he shouldn't want me. I'm the predator in his midst. A demon of my own kind.

I will help him tame his beast because I believe his cause is sound, but I want something in return.

And I always get what I want.

Chapter Twelve

As promised, later the next afternoon, Theron arrives to escort me to my new studio. When I enter, I gasp in surprise.

The room is larger than I expected—at least two times the size of my shop, with warm wooden floors and grey stone walls lined with dozens of dark wooden shelves. Hundreds of small bottles and vials filled with every herb, spice, or magical ingredient I could possibly need cover every available surface. A tall bank of windows dominates one wall, filtering in the warm afternoon light. Stretched in front is a long wooden worktable with tools and scales, burners, and beakers for measuring, heating, mixing, and slicing.

A pristine black leather bench sits on the far side of the room, perfect for practicing my craft. The smooth mechanism moves it up and down, allowing me to lift and lower the head. Next to that is another table covered in needles of every size and material, along with a shelf filled with ink bottles of at least a hundred different colors. To add to that, plants sit on top of the shelves, long vines of greenery cascading down, making the entire room feel alive.

There is absolutely no way the king managed all of this after dinner last night.

"This is incredible," I say as I take a turn around the room, trailing my hand along the shelves.

"If there's anything else you need, His Majesty is happy to provide it," Theron says.

I stop and look around the room. "Thank you. Can you send my meals here? I think I'll stay for a while."

"Of course," he says. "And His Majesty will be along shortly."

"Thank you," I say again as he bows, leaving me alone to explore. I head to a bookshelf filled with volumes on healing and various other cures. Some I've seen before, but many are entirely new to me. At this rate, I might have to order a cot brought in so I can sleep here, though that tattoo bench looks soft enough to act as a bed.

When I try out the mechanism, it's obvious how sturdy and well-made it is. This is so much nicer than what I have back at home. If I'm not mistaken, I think the king is attempting to impress me with all this. It works just a little bit.

While I wait for Ferran to arrive, I grab some of the

books and head to the workbench, pulling up the stool and flipping through them. I've been considering everything he told me last night, and we'll need to experiment. While I have plenty of practice at turning men into beasts, I've never been asked to tame one. The kings of my past had no interest in suppressing their baser animal instincts.

I'm unsure how much time passes before I hear the scuff of a boot on the floor before I look up to find the king standing in the doorway.

"Sorry, I didn't want to disturb you," he says.

"No, it's okay," I say, gesturing for him to enter. "I was doing some reading. We'll have to try a few things to get this right. I admit, it's not something I've done before."

"Of course," he says. "Do you think you can do it, though?"

While I *think* I can do it, I'm not a hundred percent sure. Magic doesn't always obey the rules as nicely as I'd like, so all we can do is try.

"Of course, I can," I say with complete confidence, thanks to the weak thread of hope in his voice. There's no point in dashing them just yet. His shoulders drop in relief, and I'm not sure why I suddenly care about ensuring this venture is a success.

"Have a seat," I say, gesturing to my chair. "This is magnificent, by the way. All of this."

"I'm glad you like it." He walks over to the bench and sits down.

"You surely didn't do all this in one night, though?"

He smiles, the corners of his eyes crinkling in the most delicious way. "You caught me. I had it started when I found out who you were. After you gave me your list last night, I had anything that was missing added."

"You were obviously very sure you'd convince me," I say, marveling at my surroundings. I've never in all my years had a workshop as nice as this. I've had bigger and grander ones, but this room feels like slotting a piece into a perfectly sized notch.

He shrugs and gives me a cocky smile that makes a needy place deep in my stomach flutter.

I cross the room, noting the hungry sweep of his gaze. Why did he stop us last night? Is it that he doesn't want to be attracted to me? Or is there some other reason I need to dig up?

For my part, I wore something that highlights my tattoos. A reminder of who I am and that he has no power to keep me here. Not one of the sheer dresses, but a light wrap-around that leaves my arms bare, with an opening that shows off my legs when I walk. I leave my feet bare, preferring to feel the sun-warmed stones against my soles.

"You'll need to take off your shirt," I say as I stop before him. He sits up and reaches back, grasping the neck and pulling it off in one smooth movement. My pussy throbs delicately because why is that so hot?

He tosses his tunic aside, and I do my best not to ogle.

He's as magnificent as I imagined he would be, all chiseled muscle and contoured lines. Except for the traces of some faded scars, I'm working with an entirely blank canvas of warm, bronzed skin.

"Lie back," I say. I adjust the mechanical bed so he's sitting at about a forty-five-degree angle, and then I study him.

I could pretend this is a professional assessment, but this is purely for my personal enjoyment. My appreciative gaze travels the dips of his exquisite collarbone and the bricks of his strong chest, wandering down the ridges of his abs and those irresistible hip muscles my fingers itch to touch. I eye the trail of dark hair that disappears into his waistband, and I make no effort to hide the fact that I'm studying the outline of his cock pressing against his pants. I felt how big he was last night, and my mouth practically waters at the idea of him filling me up.

I look back at his face to see him watching me expectantly before I wink.

"Just figuring out where we should start," I say.

After moving to his other side, I tinker with my ingredients, taking a pinch of golden clove, mixing it with sanguine blossom, and crushing them before stirring the paste with some black ink.

"Tell me about your beast form," I say. "The control in my art is based on the accuracy of my images. What does it look like?"

"Well, I've never looked in the mirror," he says. "But I

have seen my reflection in the water, and I have a lot of hair. It's dark. Almost black with some lighter brown streaks in between. I have many sharp teeth, and my hands and feet grow bigger and become tipped with claws."

As he talks, I scratch out a sketch on a piece of paper, focusing on the details. When he's done speaking, he falls silent as I continue drawing, filling out the gaps and shading the edges. When I'm done, I hold it up. "How's this?"

He looks at it and swallows. "Yes. That's it. That's incredible. How did you do that?"

"Many years of practice. Don't forget, I've been around for a while."

His mouth quirks up at the corner. "How long is a while?"

"Let's just say I could probably have helped your great, great, great grandfather if he'd needed it."

Sometimes, men are put off by that, but it's usually the meek ones who are intimidated by what I am. If I thought Ferran might fall into that category, I'm dead wrong because the heat in his eyes practically burns through my dress.

Ignoring that look, I arrange the items on my table and then hold up the first needle.

"Ready? This is going to sting."

"I'm ready."

I lay a hand over his heart. He's warm, and it's beating

rapidly. I want to ask what caused the faded scars covering his chest and stomach, but I resist the urge. I do take a moment to admire the smooth palette of his otherwise unblemished skin, loving that I'm about to claim it with my mark.

For the next few hours, I work on outlining an image of his beast onto his chest as he holds still, bearing the pain with far less complaining than Savryn has ever managed.

Slowly, I start to fill in the details. The more lifelike the image, the better the magic. I light the sconces around the room as night falls, tossing us in a warm glow.

"Are you getting tired?" I ask eventually. "We can continue tomorrow."

"I can go a little longer if you're okay?"

"Sure," I say. "I've got a little more in me, and I want to work on the face."

He nods, and I lean over, pressing in the needle before I peer up at him. His eyes flick away to a spot on the wall, and there's no doubt he was just staring down the front of my dress.

"Uh, sorry," he says, his cheeks turning pink. Why is that so fucking adorable?

I smirk. "I need to get a little closer," I say, gesturing to his chest. "The details here are very fine." I place a knee on the bench. "I'm going to get on top of you if that's okay? This position offers me the best angle."

He nods. "That's okay."

"Perfect."

This morning, I had every intention of seducing him, so I made the calculated move of 'forgetting' to put on underwear. As I straddle his torso, I shift the fabric of my skirt so that my bare pussy settles on his stomach. He lets out a sharp breath, telling me he's realized it.

"Comfortable?" I ask innocently, and he nods.

"Very." The word sounds a little strangled.

"Good." Then, I bend over and continue my work, piercing his flesh and wiping away the blood with each prick of the needle. He shudders every once in a while, clearly trying to hold in the pain.

"You're doing great," I say, and he lets out a skeptical huff.

I keep adding more ink, and his hips move under me, the trail of fine hairs on his lower torso tickling my clit and making my stomach wind tighter.

"How are you feeling?" I ask casually as he stares at me under hooded lids.

"I'm starting to understand what you were talking about. The pain and pleasure thing. When it's done by the right person."

I smile as I peer up at him through my lashes. While I was working, his hands slid to my knees. They slowly drag up my thighs as I rub myself against his stomach, wondering if he notices how wet I am.

"Do you?" I ask, digging in the needle again as I shift

myself back, settling over his cock. Oh yes, he's definitely feeling this too.

His hands slide higher, his palms both soft and rough at the same time. I sit back and allow my fingers to explore the planes of his chest, caressing all that exposed skin. I avoid the tender areas where my needle has been, and he lets out a soft groan as I drag my fingers down the lines of his stomach.

That low rumble vibrates up my spine, raising the hairs on my arms. The way he's looking at me, like a man wandering the desert without shade, makes my core throb. His hands slide higher, scooping under the fabric of my dress, his large palms resting on my skin while the pads of his fingertips dig gently into my flesh.

His thumbs sweep out, massaging the tendon right at the joints of my thighs, so close and yet much too far from where I want him. I grind down against him, and he moans, his head falling back as he presses his thumbs harder.

"Look at me," I demand, and he lifts his head, his hungry gaze following my every movement as I reach for the tie on my dress.

"Fuck," he says as I let the dress fall open and then slip it off my shoulders, leaving me completely naked. "Fuck, you're beautiful."

I roll my hips, balancing myself with my hands on his chest.

"Touch me," I say, and he pauses only for a moment

before his nostrils flare, and his hands move inwards until his thumbs finally find my wet cunt.

He moans, licking his lips as one of his thumbs finds my clit. His other hand reaches up to cup my breast before he pinches my nipple hard enough to send a shock ricocheting through my body. My back arches as I breathe out a needy gasp.

He flips his hand and cups my pussy, his thumb once again circling my clit. My legs tense as his middle finger slips along my wet center and then dips inside.

"Oh gods," I gasp as he pumps in and out.

"Ride my hand," he says in a rough voice. "Come for me, beautiful witch."

I do as he asks, rolling back and forth as he continues thrusting his fingers. His hard cock rubs against my ass as my release winds tighter and tighter. As he presses down on my clit, I shatter on a whimpering exhale. He continues touching me, drawing out the sensation before he eases out and lets out a soft grunt, his head dropping back before I collapse on top of him. I watch as he brings his fingers to his mouth and sucks them clean.

When he's done, I reach between us, sliding my hand over his thick cock, finding the fabric of his pants wet. I arch an eyebrow.

"Was that me or you?" I ask.

"A little of both, I think," he says with a sheepish smile. "That was fucking hot…" He trails off, letting out a soft sound of contentment.

I lift myself to look into his eyes, and he reaches up to tuck a lock of my hair back in a strangely gentle gesture.

"Are you too tired for more?" I ask.

Though I've been working all day, I'm only getting started on all the filthy things I want this man to do to me. I lean down to kiss him, but he recoils, something dark flashing in his eyes before he says, "Yes. Sorry. I'm sorry. I shouldn't have done that."

He's pushing himself into a sitting position as he carefully moves me off him. Again.

"What?" I ask as he swings his legs over the side of the bench and then bends to retrieve his tunic.

"Is it okay if I put this on?" He gestures to the tattoos on his chest.

"I need to bandage it before you leave."

"It's fine. I'll ask my usual healer to do it."

"No. I'll do it," I say, sliding off the bench and claiming my dress. I shove my arms into the holes, but he's already halfway out the door.

"It's fine. I'll see you tomorrow."

And then, before I can protest, he's gone.

Chapter Thirteen

I try not to let it bother me, but I do have *some* feelings. He was obviously into it during the moment, but the way he rushed off stings.

When he arrives the next day, he won't meet my eyes. We don't acknowledge it, letting it hang in the air. This isn't normally my style. I prefer just to say what's on my mind and get all unpleasantness out in the open, but my instincts say something else is bothering him, and this isn't actually about me.

But I might also just want that to be true.

What is wrong with me? When have I ever cared about what a man thinks?

While an awkward silence hangs in the room, we continue working. I ask him to recount what he sees in his beast form, including the moments with the villagers when he loses control. Thanks to the long pauses and the way he rubs the spot between his eyes, it's clear he's struggling through this conversation, but I need a visual as a guide.

I won't recreate those memories with the same accuracy as his beast—I don't want him living with the mutilated bodies of the people he hurt branded on his skin—so I focus on the abstract by asking him to describe how he felt. Sketching at my table, I use shadows and light to convey the emotions of loss and regret I hear in his voice.

Then, we continue with the ink.

Though we avoid discussing what happened between us, I've also forced him to recount all his worst moments and mistakes. So, we let the incident sink to the back, settling into a conversation between friends and getting to know one another.

By the end of the week, he's smiling a bit more again. A twinge of regret pinches my ribs, understanding this is all there is between us. I'm sure I'm not mistaking the heat in his gaze when I catch him looking at me, but I won't pursue him again. He made it clear he regretted it last time, and I do have my pride.

I'll finish the job as promised, and then maybe I'll take him up on his offer to build me a cottage deep in the woods. Perhaps I'll still open my shop once a week for those in need, but I would also be content to disappear and not talk to anyone for a long time.

"Okay," I finally say after I've spent about a week working. The left side of his chest and his ribs are now covered with black and grey markings, interspersed with splashes of green and red and blue. A beast roams through the dark trees as the shadows swirl around him. I've used an extract of uyiaran and devil moss to infuse magic into the markings, hopefully offering him the ability to control this thing that lives within. I'm not one hundred percent sure if it will work, but I'm hopeful.

"I think that's all I can do for now. We'll have to test this out."

"Perfect," Ferran says, sitting up. He looks down at the tattoo, twisting so he can get a better look. I hand him a mirror, and he studies it with a thoughtful expression. "It's incredible. You're a true master."

I smile and go about tidying up my studio.

"Did you do all of yours?" he asks, gesturing to me.

No longer intent on seducing him, I've been dressing far more modestly, though my tunic still bares my arms, offering me freedom of movement.

"Most of them," I say. "I had a teacher who helped me in the spaces I couldn't reach myself." Then I turn away because I don't want him asking any more questions about my marks, especially those that are a reminder of the worst of my sins.

"We should go into the forest tonight," I say, trying to redirect the conversation.

"That's perfect. I'm due to check on the Shadow Border anyway. My sentries say the demons are stirring again."

Later that evening, I make my way down to the front hall of the castle with Celeste in tow. We're both wearing practical clothing—leather leggings and thick tunics with boots, perfect for traipsing into the brush.

When Ferran sees me approaching, his dark eyebrows pull together. "Where are you going?"

"With you," I say before he detaches himself from the group of soldiers he was speaking with. Percy stands with them also, having recovered from the balcony incident. *Unfortunately.*

"No, it's not safe. You're staying here."

I roll my eyes and then pat him on the cheek. "It's adorable that you care about my safety." *Despite the fact you finger fucked me into oblivion, only to run out of the room and pretend it never happened.*

I scoot around him and fling open the doors. "Off we go!" I call, twirling my finger in the air. "We've got a curse to control."

I stomp down the path that leads into the forest. I took a good walk around yesterday to get a sense of my surroundings.

Ferran catches up to me. "Vespera, this isn't a good idea. You could get hurt."

"Are you kidding me?" I ask. "Do you forget who and what I am? Don't pull that alpha male bullshit with me. There's nothing you can do that I won't be able to stop."

He presses his mouth together. "Why did you bring

the girl?" He gestures to Celeste, who's walking behind us as she surveys the forest.

"Bait," I say.

"What?" he barks out. "Absolutely not."

"Don't worry. I'll protect her. You said your beast is triggered when you catch the sight, scent, or sounds of humans. Since I don't think you want to try this near the village, this is our best option to test if my markings are working."

He practically chokes on his indignation. "And you were angry at *me* for dangling her off a ledge?"

"*You* didn't give her a choice. We've spoken at length, and she agreed to help. You should be thanking her. And when it's time for her to leave, you'll double whatever you were planning to give her."

He glances back at Celeste, who watches us, and then gives a little wave with an uncertain smile. When I approached her with my idea, I was sure she would turn me down. But she's braver than I gave her credit for.

"I've assured her that no harm will come to her," I say, and I truly believe that. I would never have brought her out here otherwise. She was surprisingly eager to help. Despite the incident on the balcony, Celeste claims Ferran has been a kind and generous employer, and she wants to help him. Plus, I think she wants to get me out of here as soon as possible, given the promise I extracted from the king on her behalf. She has a home and her promised riches to enjoy.

"I don't like this," he says, his forehead creasing, and I shrug.

"It's the best plan," I say.

"We'll use Percy," he suggests. "Or one of my guards."

"They'll be busy with the demons, and surely, the scent of a sweet, innocent girl is far more appealing to your beast than that foul creature of a man who probably needs a bath...or several?"

Ferran's eyes darken before he raises an eyebrow. "I can think of something that smells much more appealing." His gaze sweeps over me, his meaning clear.

My glare turns icy because how dare he try to flirt with me?

I ignore the comment because I have no idea how to respond for once in my life. I hate how this Feral King is twisting me up. I shouldn't care what *any* man thinks or wants, and *this* one is no exception, no matter how weak my knees go in his presence.

Finally, we reach a small clearing surrounded by trees. Shadows crawl through the dense brush, making Celeste's eyes go wide. She might be regretting her decision right now.

"It's okay," I assure her. "They won't come anywhere near you. I swear it."

To prove my point, I erect a barrier around us. Nearly translucent, it shimmers dimly in the falling light. Only Ferran and his beast will have the ability to pass through.

"Okay, go," I say to him. "Do whatever it is you do."

He stares at me, indecision clear in his expression as his gaze flicks to Celeste and then returns to me. I'm not sure why he's being so reticent—he's the one who dangled her off a balcony.

Clearly realizing he won't change my mind, he reaches back, pulls off his shirt, and then strips off his pants. Gods, he's magnificent. His new tattoo gleams in the moonlight, practically alive on his skin. I did an amazing job, if I do say so myself. I just hope the proportions of pearl mace are right.

I absolutely do not ogle the impressiveness of his heavy cock hanging between his legs, and my thighs absolutely don't clamp together as I imagine it pounding into me as I cling to his arms for dear life. Celeste's eyes have grown increasingly wide, and she looks away from the king, fixating on a distant point.

Shit. Now I'm even more disappointed he rejected me. Maybe I can sneak into the village and track down Savryn, both to scold him for blabbing about my gifts and, more importantly, to relieve this constant needy ache.

Ferran turns around, showing off his perfectly round ass, before he turns to look at me with a strange expression. Then, he breaks into a slow jog before disappearing into the trees. Celeste and I wait in the clearing as the sky grows darker, listening to the distant snarling sounds of Ferran and his soldiers slaying the Shadow Demons. Their screams fill the air, and I touch a trembling Celeste on the shoulder.

"It's going to be fine. I promise I won't let anything happen to you." She gives me a tight smile and nods.

"I'm going to hide in the bushes now so the king can find you. I'll be right over there."

She says nothing, but she swallows heavily before she nods again. I slip into the brush and then wait. It takes a while before the sounds of the demons start to quiet, and I hear a howl that I'm sure must be Ferran in the distance. It's a mournful but strangely beautiful sound.

A rustle in the trees draws my attention right before a massive beast bursts through the foliage. I react instantly, touching the shield tattoo on my collarbone and throwing up a barrier around Celeste as Ferran crashes into it, his bulk bouncing off the surface and flying into the air.

He lands on the ground and then immediately shifts into his human form. I jump out and glance at Celeste, who's a little pale but otherwise unharmed. Ferran rolls over with a groan, and I scoop up his discarded clothing, dropping it on top of him to cover up his very erect cock.

"Damn. That didn't work," I say, and he looks up at me. "What did you feel?"

"It did a little," he says. "I was able to resist her for a short time before the beast broke through."

I nod and consider that. That's good. "Okay. I need to tweak some things."

I spin around, grab Celeste by the hand, and drag us both to the castle.

Chapter Fourteen

Over the next few weeks, I try out a number of different combinations and concoctions to help Ferran control his beast. We're circling closer and closer to a solution as his resistance to tracking down and devouring Celeste grows stronger and stronger. But it's not enough. Eventually, he always slips. I can sense his frustrations, and the more distraught he becomes, the more I want to help him. I'm not sure why I care, but there's no use pretending I'm not fully invested in his cause.

Maybe it's because when I fell asleep in the armchair in the corner one night, I awoke with a blanket tucked around me. Or when I returned from a survey of the forests, my hands numb from the autumn air, I found a vase of fresh flowers on my worktable, along with a steaming pot of tea. Maybe it's because the kitchen makes my favorite pastries every morning while ensuring dinner consists of my favorite meals.

I'm sure Ferran is responsible for all these touches, but neither of us acknowledges them. Are they simply kind gestures to thank me for my help, or do they mean something more? He's made no further attempts to advance our physical relationship, so I chalk them up to platonic tokens of appreciation and suppress my disappointment. He's just one man, and there will be plenty more after I'm done here.

After another failed attempt, we're back in the castle when I find Ferran sitting alone in the massive dining room with a bottle and a glass in front of him.

When I enter, he looks up, his gaze traveling over me in that hungry way that always steals my breath. Does he realize he's doing it? I want to tell him to knock it off, but I also derive a masochistic kind of pleasure in his attention. I'm not used to pining for anyone, and I'm not sure I like it.

"Hi," I say, sitting next to him and helping myself to a sip of his drink. "You okay?"

"It's not working," he says. "I'm not strong enough."

"We're getting there. I'm going to figure this out."

"It's not you," he replies, dropping his head in his hands, his elbows planted on the table. "It's me. No magic in the world is strong enough to fight this weakness within me."

"First of all, I take offense to your lack of faith in my abilities," I say, and he looks up with an almost smile.

"Second of all, this is powerful magic we're dealing with. Whoever cursed your father was a real bitch. No one, no matter how strong, could be expected to control this on their own."

Ferran sighs and reaches for the glass, our fingers brushing, sending a bolt of heat straight to my stomach. He pauses for a moment before he takes a long pull.

"Why are you trying to make me feel better?" he says, his gaze searching me. "I don't deserve this after everything I've done to you. I don't deserve *you*."

I blink at his words, wondering if that's what all of this is about.

"You seem genuine in your desire to help your kingdom," I say. "Most kings I've known aren't like that. Most are too obsessed with their egos and need for authority to give much thought to the people they rule."

"Have you known many kings?" he asks.

"Way more than I'd like," I say with a wry tone, and he laughs, the warm sound filling the room. "Anyway, I have another idea. I'm not sure if it will work, but it's worth a shot."

"What is it?"

"As a precaution, I put a marking on you that matches one of mine. It can tether us so I can feel what you feel in your beast form. It might give me a clearer picture of how to control this once and for all."

"That seems dangerous," he says, understandably wary.

"It will only be temporary. I'll use a form of ink that wears off after about a week. The catch, of course, is that I'll be able to feel you, whether you're in your beast form or not."

"What do you mean by feel me?"

"I mean, I'll be able to sense your emotions. I won't be able to hear your thoughts or anything, but I'll be able to understand a lot about what's going on in there." I point to his heart, and he looks down before looking back up. "Of course, if you're uncomfortable with that, I understand. Most people are wary about giving up that much control. You have to really trust the one tethering you."

"I trust you," he says immediately. "Absolutely."

I don't know why those earnest words make my heart twist, but they unlock a hard ball of emotion in my chest. I try to push past, ignoring it, because these feelings are useless, and I'll soon be gone from this place.

I nod. "Then you want to try it?"

"Yes. Whatever you need. I'll try anything."

I take in a deep breath. "Okay, I'll get everything ready. I'm going to need your help, though. It's in a spot I can't reach myself."

His brows draw together. "I can't draw," he says. "At all."

I laugh at how serious he is about that. "It's okay.

You'll just be tracing what's already there. It's a very simple design."

"Anything you need," he repeats, his gaze intense, as though he's trying to send me a message.

"Okay, then I'll see you in the morning."

I push myself up and head for the door when Ferran calls out.

"Vespera." I stop and turn. "Thank you. For all of this. Nothing I give you can ever make up for your help."

There's such emotion in his voice that a lump forms in my throat. I don't dare speak, worried I'll betray myself with this messy tangle of emotions, so I tip my head and turn around to leave.

Chapter Fifteen

The next morning, Ferran finds me in my workshop. I've readied the ink for the tethering tattoo, mixing the ingredients with a heavy dash of hope. I've never been a hundred percent sure if I can find the answer he needs, but I'm determined to do my best.

"Hi," he says, filling the space with his magnetic energy. Our eyes meet, and neither of us moves for a moment until I look away, breaking the contact, my neck flushing with heat. I need to stop letting him affect me this way.

"Morning," I say, focusing on my workbench. I pour the ink I've just mixed into a small glass jar and then carry it to my table. "I have the ink ready, so we can get started."

"Okay," Ferran says, rubbing his hands together.

"What do you need me to do? I never imagined I'd become an artist during all this."

The corner of my mouth ticks up at his enthusiasm. His radiant smile makes my chest ache in a way I don't think I like. If this doesn't work, I'll have to concede this problem is beyond my abilities. Either way, I want to finish this so I can get as far away from here as possible. I also don't like how much I think about him. How I miss him even when he's standing right in front of me. I didn't sign up for any of this.

"Okay, well, as I said, it's in a bit of an awkward spot."

I reach under the hem of my tunic and pull off my leggings as Ferran's eyes widen.

"The inside of my thigh," I say by way of explanation. He nods, his eyes never leaving me as I cross the room and hop onto the bench.

"Sit down," I say, pointing to the wheeled stool at the foot of the table. "You'll want to do it from this end."

He moves slowly like he's a fly caught in tree sap. Dropping into the seat, he maneuvers it so he's at my feet, and I scoot down.

"This needle," I say, picking one up from the small table at my side. "Dip it in here and then press it on my skin here."

I bend and slide my knee up so he can see what I mean. At the very apex of my thigh is a simple tattoo of three interlocking rings. His gaze drops to where I'm pointing, and it's at that moment when I wonder if this is a terrible idea.

I'd forgotten it was so high up. It's been a long time since I've used it.

"Why is it...there?" he asks, his voice rough before he clears it and looks up at me.

"Because it ties me to another person, so it's as close as possible to the source of feminine power. The place where life begins." I try to say it in a detached, professional way, but it comes out far too breathless to be believable.

"Anyway—" I clear my throat. "—you'll use a series of dots to trace each of these lines, ensuring you keep the needle nice and straight. That's it. Very easy."

His wary gaze meets mine, and I suspect I can read what he's thinking. Maybe not so easy. I'm used to it, but most people don't have much experience piercing someone else's skin.

"Okay, sure," he says. "I think I can do that."

"Great. I suggest you use the end of the bench to stabilize your elbow and keep your hand steady."

He nods and accepts the needle before he does as I've instructed. The sharp tip slides in, and even though I've done this a million times, that familiar sting of pain ricochets through my limbs. I let out a heavy, shuddering breath, and Ferran looks up.

"Is that okay?" His brows furrow in concern.

"Yes," I say. "You're doing great."

He continues working, adding more markings as he fills out each ring. I hold so still, it's like I'm made of glass. This is torture, but not because of the pain—no, it's because I'm enjoying this way more than I should. His warm breath on my skin combines with the prick of the needle, making my pussy ache. He's concentrating so hard while the tension in the room grows thicker and thicker. His gaze lifts to meet mine, his pupils growing wide, and then, he tears it away.

He must notice the way goosebumps spread over my thighs every time he touches me.

"Is this the kind of pain you meant?" he asks suddenly, looking up. "When I touched you with the copper? Is this the same?"

"Yes," I say without really meaning to. Do I want him to know that?

He pricks me with the needle again, and I swear, he presses harder this time, making me groan. With hooded eyes, he moves his hand so his knuckles brush against my center, and stars burst behind my eyes. I'm so aroused, I must be radiating off waves of heat.

"I want to touch you again," he says, his voice raw and cracked, like he's admitting something that breaks his heart.

My head lifts so I can stare down at him. "Do you? You keep pushing me away, but then you're constantly looking at me like...that."

"I'm sorry," he breathes. "It's just, I haven't been with anyone in a very long time, and I freaked out."

Well, I wasn't expecting him to say that.

"You haven't? Why not?"

"The beast," he says. "When I'm...inside someone, it comes too close to the surface, and I can't control myself. I made that mistake once, and I can't do it again."

Oh. This explains a lot.

"How long has it been?" I ask, my eyes wide.

"Years," he says. "So *many* fucking years."

I let out a ragged breath.

"But you don't need to worry about that with me," I say, and his expression becomes a mixture of hope and swelling lust.

"I know." He rubs his hands down his face. "All those times you've stopped me from attacking Celeste made me realize you have nothing to fear from me, and I... but that's not why I want to... I mean..." His shoulders drop. "I mean, I think you're the most exciting woman I've ever met, and even if you couldn't fight off a feather, I'd desperately want to touch you right now."

I laugh softly. It might be the nicest thing anyone has said to me in a long time.

"I'll accept that," I say, and he quirks a tentative smile.

"I think I need to go slow," he says. "I'm...I need..."

"It's okay," I say, laying a hand on his shoulder. "I get it. You have some trauma to overcome. These things don't happen overnight. We can take it slow if that's what you need."

"But I want to do this." He runs a hand up my thigh as his finger teases the edge of my underwear. "I want *this* now."

I nod with my heart caught in my throat. "As long as you promise not to run away after we're done."

He lets out a low chuckle. "I promise."

"Finish first," I say, gesturing to the tattoo. "You're almost done."

"I have a better idea," he says, a wicked gleam forming in his eyes. He leans forward and runs his nose along the seam of my underwear, and I moan, leaning back on my hands as he takes a deep inhale.

"Fuck, you smell so good, beautiful witch."

He presses the needle into my skin, and my body tenses at the prick of pain. He uses his other hand to push aside the fabric between my legs before he leans forward and circles my clit with his tongue.

"Oh gods," I gasp, a moan vibrating in my chest.

He tugs on my underwear with one hand, and I lift my hips before he slides it down and tosses it away. Then, he presses his hand to the inside of my thigh to spread my legs.

He admires me for several seconds, licking his lips before he looks up. "Stay just like that. Don't move."

Then, he drives the needle in again, and my entire core tightens, the ache radiating out through my limbs.

After a few more pricks of pain, I gather he's finished because he tosses the needle aside and hooks his hands around my thighs, dragging me towards him. He buries his face into my warm, wet skin and licks me from back to front in one long, luxurious slide.

My hips buck, and he pins me down with his arm as he dives in, sucking my clit as his hand slides up to cup my breast. He squeezes it, pinching my nipple as he fucks me with his tongue. It doesn't take long for my release to climb to the surface, that tingling feeling spreading through my stomach.

"Yes!" I pant, gripping the leather beneath my hands. "Yes, like that," I beg as he continues licking and nipping, his rough stubble creating the perfect amount of friction as my hips churn, riding his face.

After another moment, my back arches, heat spreading across my lower back before I explode with a loud cry. Ferran continues eating me up, waiting for me to settle as he laps me up like he can't get enough. Finally, he pulls away and gives me a feral smile.

"Gods," he says, rubbing his chin. "That was incredible."

"For me, you mean," I say, more than a little breathless. "It seems like I'm the only one having orgasms in this workshop."

He grins. "As it should be."

He winks and stands up from the stool, placing kisses up my body until he reaches my neck, sucking on the skin at the curve of my throat. Then, he touches his forehead to mine.

"Thank you."

"I should be the one thanking you. I think I blacked out for a second."

His answering laugh is warm and light. "Thank you for giving me a second chance, or maybe it was a third one at this point? And thank you for trying so hard to find an answer for me."

I touch his face, noting that his hair is now suitably mussed. "You're welcome. I'll do everything I can."

"I know." He plants a firm kiss on my forehead and backs away. "This isn't me running away, I swear. This is me having to check on a few things before we go into the forest tonight."

I sit up. "Understood."

"We're good?"

"We're great," I reply, and his shoulders relax.

"Okay, then I'll see you in a few hours?"

"Of course."

"Thank you, Vespera."

He takes my hand and kisses my palm, the press of his warm lips lingering on my skin. A moment later, he's gone.

Chapter Sixteen

Over the next two nights, we gather in the forest, surrounded by the changing leaves, the cool air nipping at our noses and cheeks. I pay close attention to Ferran's moods and emotions when he shifts. What I'm searching for is that exact moment when the beast takes over. What is he feeling? What is he thinking? Where is the slip? We're getting so close. He's so frustrated, but I do my best to be encouraging. I'm still not certain I can do this, but the solution feels within reach.

During the day, I spend hours in my workshop, mixing, grinding, and testing various combinations until I think I'm getting it right. In the afternoons, Ferran visits me, usually bearing some kind of gift—a tin of my favorite tea or a bottle of the sparkling faerie wine I love that I know is impossible to find around these parts—as I add more details to the story I'm drawing over his skin.

When he lies on my bench, shirtless and looking good enough to eat, I fight the urge to straddle him or return the favor and suck on his cock. I agreed to take this slow and don't want to make any sudden movements. But it's testing all of my patience.

What's happening to me? Why am I treating him with kid gloves? Normally, I'd have tossed him aside and gone in search of someone who could handle me. I think about Savryn and realize that not only have I lost the urge to be with him, but the idea makes me a little queasy. I am eager to return to my shop, though. I find I miss the bustle and the conversations of my days. I *like* helping the villagers with their ailments.

The tether with Ferran is making it harder and harder to resist him because I can sense everything he's feeling, including his desire, *especially* his desire. He's holding himself back, and I must respect that he needs space to confront his inner demons.

The other night, he admitted that he nearly killed the last woman he had sex with, and it was only by a miracle intervention from his healer that she survived. It was far too close for comfort, and that was when he walled himself off entirely from all physical relationships.

Ferran is back in my workshop as I make a few more tweaks before we head into the forest tonight. While I'm working, a wave of his acute longing hits me in the gut, causing my hands to shake.

"Can you stop that?" I ask. "I can feel everything you're feeling." I widen my eyes to try to drive the point home. I couldn't be more wrong if I think I might embarrass him. His handsome face cracks into the first smile I've seen in days.

"It's not my fault you're the most fucking gorgeous thing I've ever seen."

As my cheeks heat, I roll my eyes, strangely giddy at the comment. It's not like I haven't heard these sentiments before. A bit of skin. A bit of makeup. The right dress to accentuate your curves and these types of compliments are easy to drag out of simple-minded men.

But I'm a mess right now, burning the candle at every end, trying to find a solution. And when Ferran says it, it feels like he'd say it no matter how I was dressed. The sentiments feel different coming from him.

Goddess, I need to get my shit together.

"I'm trying to focus," I say, and he grins as he lays back, tucking an arm under his head, accentuating the curve of his bicep.

"Okay. I'll think of decidedly unsexy things," he says solemnly. "Like math equations and how Percy picks his teeth when he's eating." Ferran snaps his fingers. "Oh, I've got it. Marigold's bunions."

I snort out a laugh, and he chuckles as I smack him playfully. "Stop that. You're not helping."

"Fine. I'll lie here and shut up, then?"

"I do like my men to be quiet," I quip, and a stumbling blip of emotion pulses through the tether. I just called him mine. The tips of my ears grow hot, and I clear my throat.

"Okay, I'm almost done," I say, my voice tight. "We'll try this out tonight. I have a good feeling."

He lets me work, though it's wildly obvious he's *not* thinking about Marigold's bunions. Still, I do my best to focus.

When I'm finished, I send him on his way so I can get a few hours of sleep on the cot in the corner before we head out. I'll miss this space when it's time to go home, and I've decided to use some of my payment from the king to renovate my apothecary into something similar.

Later that night, I gather with Celeste, Ferran, Percy, and a selection of his guards in the front hall before we make our usual procession into the forest. Due to our constant presence, the cover of demons has been thin lately, and it takes less than an hour for Ferran and his men to dispense with any lurking in the trees.

As usual, Celeste waits in the clearing, singing with a high, bright voice that floats through the air like an angel tempting the devil into heaven. She's like a cherry lollipop spinning in the middle of a group of toddlers, but I know Ferran can do this.

After a few minutes, a rustle in the trees signals his

approach, and Celeste's voice falters at the sound. Despite the dangers, I believe she's become reasonably confident that I won't let anything happen to her. There have been a few near misses, but she's come out of these experiments completely unharmed. And I intend to keep it that way. Thanks to her not-annoying company and constant supply of smutty books, we've become closer than I'd ever have imagined.

Another rustle draws our attention, and Celeste's voice tapers off as she clutches the hem of her tunic. Then, there he is. Ferran steps through the trees slowly, his breath fogging the air. I've seen him this way many times, but the sight still makes me go quiet. He's so powerful in his beast form. He's already a large man, but like this, he's larger than life. Bulging muscles and fur and teeth. All snarls and wild energy. It's no wonder those villagers never stood a chance.

He prowls forward, taking one tentative step after another, his bright eyes glowing with the faintest trace of yellow in the moonlight. Celeste steps back as he moves closer, but I wait because the energy siphoning through the tether feels different. He's not mindless and drooling. He no longer bounds into the clearing without a second thought. I sense he's still in control, so I hold back, giving him the chance he needs.

He lets out a rumbling huff, his wide chest expanding, and then he shakes his head before he turns around and bounds away. I let out a cry of triumph as I leap out of the bushes. Closing my eyes, I feel for him. He's running and still in control—just barely, but he did it.

I feel his joy through the tether as a triumphant howl echoes through the still night.

Chapter Seventeen

Ferran isn't willing to concede success just yet, however. He insists we keep trying, over and over. He resists Celeste again and then again, becoming stronger and stronger each time. I feel his triumph through the tether and the tangle of emotions he's clinging to so tightly whenever he looks at me. There's no question the beast makes him feral in more ways than one, as evidenced by how hard he is whenever he returns to his human form.

With the ability to sense his emotions, the whole process is making me a little wild and desperate with longing. Thankfully, I have Celeste's books to keep me company while he sorts out the thoughts in his head.

Tonight, Celeste and I wait in a clearing we chose for its proximity to one of the villages in the valley. Ferran is somewhere out there, and I sense his control. He's aware of his surroundings. Aware of Celeste. Aware of the village, close enough that its distant sounds reach us. He isn't tempted to head in their direction, and I'm so proud of him, I could burst.

Ferran takes his time, circling nearer and nearer to the village. They have no idea how close they all are to their deaths, but he's fine. His thoughts are clear and whole. He tests himself, looping around the perimeter for a long time until, finally, he enters the clearing. He looks at Celeste with those dark beast eyes and then shakes his head before he transforms back into a human. His gaze finds mine instantly, and I run over, throwing my arms around his neck as he spins me around.

"I did it!" he says.

"You did it!"

I frame his face with my hands, and he leans down to press his nose into the curve of my neck, a low rumble vibrating in his chest. A crest of desire slams into me, and I inhale a sharp breath, so desperate for him that my entire body is trembling.

"Ves," he rumbles softly.

"Yes?" I whisper before he looks behind his shoulder at Percy and his guards.

"Take Celeste back to the castle," he orders them. "Now."

No one wastes a moment, disappearing from the clearing before Ferran picks me up, my legs wrapping around his waist.

"I'm ready," he says, his eyes dark with lust. "I can't take it anymore. I want you so much, I'm going to fucking die if I can't have you."

"Oh, thank the goddess," I answer. "I was going to lose my mind if I had to wait any longer." My back hits a tree, and he grinds his thick cock against me as I moan.

"I have a hunting cabin nearby," he says, his voice strangled. "We should..." He can't seem to speak as he thrusts against me again.

"Sure," I breathe. "Anywhere. I don't care. Just fuck me. Please." The words come out as more of a whimper than a demand, but Ferran has a way of stripping away all my defenses. I need him *now*.

I push him back and then slide down, turning him so he's backed against the tree. Stretching up onto my tiptoes, I kiss his throat, then his collarbone, the flat planes of his chest where my beast tattoo covers his skin, and then I fall to my knees.

"Fuck," he shudders as I rake my nails down his thighs, looking up before I grip his cock in my hand. His hips move as I pump him for a few seconds and then place the wide head in my mouth, sucking on the tip. He moans as his head falls back, his entire body quivering with the threadbare restraint he's been clinging to for so many years.

"Oh gods," he says. "Fuck, it's been so long. I'm not going to last..."

"It's okay," I say. "We've got all night."

He smiles down at me as his hand slides under my hair, a wild glint in his eyes. "Then hold still because I'm going to fuck your mouth like I'm a dying man."

I open my mouth to accept him. He's so big that I'm pushed to my limit, wondering if all that will fit. But goddess, I'll try my best.

Then, he's moving, his hips thrusting, the tip hitting the back of my throat. The sounds he makes are not unlike the beast he's been trying so hard to tame. I dig my fingers into his thighs as I hold on. His hand twists my hair tight enough to burn my scalp, causing my clit to throb with the need to be touched.

He thrusts in and out until my eyes run with tears, and then I feel him thicken before he lets out a shuddering groan and fills my mouth. I swallow him down as he slows his pace, finally pulling out with a ragged sigh.

He falls to his knees, cupping my face in his hands and kissing my cheeks as he wipes away my tears. "Are you okay?" he asks. "I think I..."

"You were fine," I promise. "You were in control the whole time. I felt it."

He smiles in a carefree, boyish way that does something to my heart. "Come on," he says. "It's getting cold out here, and I'm not done with you yet."

He scoops me up, carrying me through the woods, and it doesn't take long to find a small but cozy-looking house nestled in the trees. He opens the door, and we're on each other instantly. He tears at my clothes, and he's conveniently already naked.

I land on the bed, and he falls to his knees, jerking my hips forward so he can run his tongue along my aching pussy. With my legs hooked over his shoulders, he feasts on me for a minute before he pulls away and flips me onto my stomach. His warm lips travel up the curve of my ass and the middle of my back until he finds my throat, sucking on the skin hard enough to make me gasp. Then, I feel the blunt head of his cock pressing against my entrance, his hands gripping my hips.

"Is this okay?" he asks, his voice breathless. I can feel him shaking, and I press my hips back.

"Yes, goddess. Please. Ferran, I want you."

He eases in, slowly sliding in the tip, and fuck, I'm already so full. He's thick and heavy, and it takes some maneuvering to accommodate him. He drives in an inch, and I cry out before he stops, waiting for me to adjust. Then he thrusts in a little further, and I grip the bed sheets as I groan. Goddess, in all my years, I don't think I've ever had a cock that felt this fucking magnificent.

"Tell me if it's too much," he says, and I shake my head.

"No, keep going." He slides a bit further until he's fully seated. He pauses as we both catch our breath.

He kisses the arch of my neck and then pulls his hips back slowly before he slams them forward. I cry out as he fills me again, warmth tingling straight to the tips of my fingers. He strokes in and out, his cock hitting every nerve ending until I'm not sure how much more I can take. Without warning, he yanks me up so my back is flush with his front as he continues to thrust into me. His hand slides down my stomach before finding my clit, which he circles with his finger while his other hand wraps around my throat, his lips finding my cheek as he whispers filthy things in my ear.

"That's a girl," he rumbles. "Gods, you feel so fucking good. So fucking tight and wet. This is the most perfect little pussy I've ever fucked."

Who is this king? This man who hasn't claimed anyone in so long?

"I'm going to make you come," he growls as he thrusts again and rubs my clit. I come apart as he squeezes my throat tight enough to make me lightheaded. Waves of shuddering pleasure spread through my limbs as he continues thrusting harder and harder. He pushes me back on my stomach and then pumps in and out, his back pressed against mine.

It's then I can feel the beast rising inside him, trying to take over. It opens its eyes, and its maw spreads into a wicked smile, its teeth glinting in the light. I touch the small beast head I recently tattooed on my forearm, filtering out a small ribbon of magic, and it blinks in response, melting away until there's just Ferren again, driving into me with abandon, his cock bottoming out until he moans and then releases with a shuddering groan.

"Fuck," he cries. "Oh, gods." I can feel the anguish, the relief, the absolute release of so many years of pent-up desire. He continues pumping his hips until he finally slows, collapsing on the bed next to me as he pulls me close.

"Thank you," he says with such seriousness that I start giggling. He wraps an arm around me tighter and throws a heavy leg over mine. "What are you laughing at, beautiful witch?"

"You just thanked me for sex. I don't think anyone has ever done that before."

"Well, they should be because that was…practically a religious awakening."

"Don't you know how to flatter a girl? Quit pumping up my ego."

He grins and then kisses my neck before nuzzling against it. It's then I notice that he never kisses me on the lips. I mean, I've already noticed, but I thought maybe we were working up to it. But we've just had our mouths in every other possible place, and it's starting to seem a little suspicious. Is he keeping something from me?

I flip around to face him, staring up into his eyes. He's smiling at me with such tenderness that I admonish myself for questioning him.

"I'm going to start the fire," he says. "It's cold in here. Don't move. We're doing that again."

He slides off the bed and walks over to the large fireplace on the other side of the room. Now that we've stopped moving, the sweat on my body evaporates, chilling my skin. I slide under the covers and watch as he grabs some logs and lights a match. Before long, the room is crackling with cozy warmth.

"I'm sorry," he says. "There's nothing to eat. I haven't been out here in a while, but there is whisky." He holds up the bottle and hands it to me, and I take a long sip before I wipe my mouth with the back of my hand.

"This will do," I say, and then he takes the bottle and swallows before placing it on the floor.

Then, he rolls on top of me. "Ready for round two?"

"Of how many?" I ask, arching a brow.

"I'm not sure I can count that high."

I laugh as he drops a kiss to my collarbone, and then he moves lower, his tongue finding me wet and waiting for everything he can throw my way.

Chapter Eighteen

We lose track of the hours as we explore each other again and again. While I love every moment, I can't help but notice he still hasn't kissed me. He's had his mouth on literally every inch of my body, and I'm not imagining things. What hasn't he told me?

Fire crackles in the hearth, warming the cabin, and we've been through a fair amount of whisky. I wouldn't mind a bit to eat right now, but I'm also more than sated.

"What do they all mean?" Ferran asks as his fingers gently trace the markings that cover my skin. "What about this one?"

He points to a small moon surrounded by stars tattooed on the front of my shoulder.

"This one is for seeing under the cover of night." I take his hand and slide it to my stomach, where there's an image of two swords crossing on my abdomen. "This one is for fighting. Thanks to this, I can wield a sword better than most trained soldiers."

"Why do you need a sword? You seem more than powerful enough to handle anything."

"You never know," I say. "I like to be prepared."

His hand wanders to my hip and the scar that puckers my skin where I cut out a chunk of my flesh once upon a time. A futile attempt to slice away the evidence of my sins.

"What's this?" he asks softly, as though he already understands it will be difficult for me to talk about.

I let out a deep breath. "It was a tattoo that once bound me to a king and was how I helped him transform into a monster."

I roll my neck. I've never told anyone the complete story before, but I'm suddenly seized with the desire to let it all out. It's impossible to deny I feel more than a passing interest in Ferran, and he needs to understand the very worst of the things I've done.

"I had a lover," I say, "many, many years ago. He was fae and set to inherit a crown, but his brother wanted it more. Malakar. He came to me and convinced me to banish his brother so he could take the throne. He promised me the world, and…I wanted it."

I stop, and Ferran rubs my arm, telling me he's listening.

"I used my magic to bind his brother inside a forest and put an impossible price on his freedom. We left him there for centuries." I blow out a breath. "Shortly after, Malakar took the crown, and I ignored any reservations I had."

I stop talking and Ferran remains quiet, giving me time.

"At first, I didn't care what he did with my magic. Witches are often shunned and treated like pariahs, and my life consisted mostly of hatred and prejudice. But I had all the power I'd always craved at his side. Not my magic, but the power of a nation. People respected me. Revered me. I had everyone at my command. It was intoxicating."

I break off. I've had a lot of time to think about those days, ashamed of how I let it all go to my head. Ashamed of the way I behaved, caring only about what I wanted. But Ferran watches me with no judgment in his expression, and it gives me the strength to carry on.

"After a time, I grew uncomfortable with what he was doing. Eventually, I refused to give him more power. He wanted the freedom to enter the enemy's camps and simply obliterate them where they slept, and though I believed in my country and the war we were fighting, I disagreed with methods like that. They were soldiers who also believed in the validity of their cause, just as much as we did. I'm no saint, but even for me, it all became too much."

He runs his fingers along the scar, waiting for me to continue.

"So, I took a knife to myself and cut out the marking that bound us." I gesture to my hip. "He was furious. He threw me in a cage made of copper, where I languished for months." I swallow as Ferran's hand tightens against my hip, anger flashing in his gaze. "He made me strip naked and then placed the cage right in the middle of the soldier's camp, where they'd stare at me and hurl every vile insult and innuendo you can possibly imagine. Still, I refused to reconnect the bond. I refused to give him back his beast."

"Then what?" he asks, his body trembling with barely contained fury.

"A guard took pity on me," I say. "One night, when the camp was quiet, he opened the lock and walked away. He said nothing, and I never knew who he was. If he'd been caught, I can't imagine what Malakar would have done to him, but I'll forever be grateful there was one man brave enough to do the right thing, even if I didn't really deserve it.

"I found some clothes stolen from an empty tent. They were far too big, but I didn't care. I just wanted to be covered, and once I was sure no one had seen me, I ran."

Ferran is hanging on to every word as I recount this tale.

"But Malakar wanted me back. He hunted me for years. I could never remain in one place for too long.

There were countless moments when his men came so close to finding me, and I escaped by the skin of my teeth more times than I care to imagine. I reinvented myself over and over, taking on new names and personas, and I studied. I learned everything I could about my magic so I'd never be vulnerable to anyone ever again. I swore I would never serve another king for as long as I lived. In the end, no matter how worthy their cause, I understood they'd always become twisted by what I could offer. Power invariably destroys the minds of men."

I look up at him, and he's studying me with his jaw hard.

"Does he still live?" Ferran asks.

I shake my head. "No. After years of running, I heard he died, and it was the first time in years that I could breathe."

"How did he die? Fae are immortal, are they not?"

I nod. "It was his brother. He found a way to break the curse I put on him and returned to reclaim his throne and his life." I smile at the thought. "I've always hoped he's happy. He didn't deserve any of what we did to him. Shortly after that, I found my way to Twilight's End, where I set up shop, changed my name again, and hoped it would be the last time."

"I'm so sorry," Ferran says, taking my hand and gathering my fingers as he kisses the tips. "You didn't deserve that either."

I give him a rueful smile. "But I did. I deserved a lot of it."

"We all do things we aren't proud of sometimes," he says.

"Like kidnapping me?" I ask with an arch of my brow.

"Something like that," he answers with a half smile.

"How did Percy break into my shop, anyway?"

He tips his head. "Percy might be many things, but the fucker can pick a lock like no one's business."

I laugh and then pull his head down for a kiss.

He recoils, jerking back.

"Okay, what is going on?" I say, sitting up. "Why won't you kiss me?"

"I've been kissing you all night," he says.

"I mean on my mouth!"

Guilt flashes across his expression, and I leap for him, trying to press my lips to his. Still, he backs away, scrambling off the bed.

"What are you keeping from me? I've been bending over backward trying to help you, and this is how you repay me?"

His shoulders slump, a shadow of regret passing over his expression.

"I haven't been completely honest with you about the curse," he finally says, and that's when I'm sure.

"I made a joke about breaking it," I say. "True love's kiss."

Ferran nods miserably, dropping his face in his hands.

"The curse is broken by true love's kiss."

"How do you know that?"

"The mage told my father."

"But why didn't he just kiss your mother then?"

Ferran snorts. "I love both of my parents, but theirs was a marriage of convenience. They were never in love. I think my mother tried, but my father never returned those feelings. Though she's never said it out loud, I think her loveless existence made my mother deeply unhappy. She was always a romantic at heart—she liked those books you enjoy reading, too. Seeing how much it pained my mother when she *couldn't* break the curse was heartbreaking."

My brow furrows as I sift through this new information. "But for any of this to matter, you'd have to be in love with me," I say, and he stands up, pacing the room, avoiding my gaze.

"Are you...in love with me?" I whisper the words, but they echo in the small cabin with the force of trumpets. Ferran stops, and it's impossible to read the expression on his face. He shakes his head and huffs a dry laugh before approaching the bed and crouching in front of me.

"I love you, Ves. How can you not see that? Feel it in my every thought and emotion? Every time you're around me. Every time you touch or look at me, can you not feel what I feel?"

I swallow a growing lump in my throat. "I thought

that was lust," I say, and the corner of his mouth crooks up before he takes my hand.

"What I feel for you goes so much deeper than that. I never thought I could feel this way."

I'm not sure how to respond to that.

"And you're wrong. It doesn't matter if I'm in love with you. What matters is if you're in love with me, too. I've been resisting the desire to kiss you because I didn't want to risk anything. I know it was too much to hope, but the curse breaks only if we both feel that way."

He's breathing heavily, his broad chest heaving as he watches me with a mixture of raw emotion and vulnerability in his eyes. I open my mouth and shake my head, already knowing the answer to the question he's too afraid to ask. But he doesn't need to be afraid.

"I love you too," I whisper, knowing I've been dancing around this truth. I do. It's been so many years since I let anyone in, but this king who kidnapped and tried to torture me has revealed a side that has drawn me in, bit by bit. I can't fault him for what he did—I would have done the same had our positions been reversed. I've done so much worse.

"I love you too," I say again, this time more forcefully. He smiles before he bends forward and wraps his arms around my waist, burying his face against me. We stay like that for a minute before he pulls away.

Then, I punch him in the shoulder. Hard.

"Ow! What was that for?" He rubs the spot, frowning at me.

"Did it never occur to you that while I was frantically hunting for a solution to your problems, this information might have been important!?"

He blinks. "I...didn't think of that."

"No. Clearly not."

I push him off me and start pacing the length of the room.

"Ves," he says, and I ignore him as I turn over these bits of knowledge in my head. "Vespera!"

"What?" I say, spinning around to face him.

"I love you," he says, spreading his hands wide.

"Yes. So you've said."

"And you love me."

"Right?"

He presses his mouth together. "Can you...stop the curse from breaking?"

"Goddess," I say, rubbing my face. It's been a hundred years since I've allowed myself to feel anything for someone, and it's already slipping away. He managed to hold off the beast tonight, but can he do it again? How do I ensure this control is permanent?

"I don't know."

His shoulders drop before he sits down on the bed.

"When I ordered Percy to kidnap you, I just wanted to find a way to control it." I settle next to him as he continues talking. "I never imagined I'd fall in love with you. I've spent so many years never allowing myself to get close to anyone. I knew that I could never be physical with anyone, and allowing someone into my heart was dangerous. But then you appeared, and no matter how I tried to resist, I couldn't stay away from you. I wanted you from the moment I saw you, but I never dared hope you might return my feelings."

I blow out a breath. "Why did you have to be…" I wave a hand in his direction. "Charming?"

He grins at that. "You're rather charming yourself."

"Charming," I huff. "I am irresistible."

He laughs. "I can't disagree with that."

"So you want me to help you control the beast *and* find a way to ensure the curse can't be broken so I can kiss you?"

"Well, I'm the one who's going to kiss you, but essentially, yes."

"I'm the one doing the kissing," I say, and his grin widens.

"We'll discuss it."

I give him a wry smile and then shake my head.

"I need to go back to my workshop."

Chapter Nineteen

I cloister myself within my workshop's walls, flipping through books and writing down lists of ingredients. My focus has shifted, and now, I need to figure out how to both bind and control the curse. I must find a way to lock it within Ferran while also allowing him the freedom to manipulate it.

He comes to see me regularly, often just sitting quietly and watching me work, always with more gifts. This is his language of love, and the trinkets piling up might have felt like clutter at another point in my life, but now, they feel like symbols of the kisses he can't give me. We've agreed not to touch each other while I sort through this new problem, and it's getting harder and harder to resist.

After several days, I finally have a breakthrough. I've found a rare herb that can create a potion to lock the curse within Ferran. It's a complicated process that will require all my skills to make it work, but I'm willing to try, for Ferran's sake.

I gather all the ingredients I need and begin the process. It's a delicate dance, mixing the components just right. Ferran watches me intently, his eyes never leaving my hands as I work.

As the concoction begins to take shape, we hover in each other's space, nearly on the edge of snapping due to the cloak of sexual tension suffocating us both. My body craves him, and I know he feels the same.

We're in my workshop on another afternoon as he sits with me, the air heavy with pressure. I look over, and Ferran's gaze grows more intense. Without a word, he takes a step towards me, his presence speaking to the primal part of me that wants to throw him to the ground and sit on his face.

He steps closer, his hand reaching out to touch mine. The connection is electric and overwhelming, and for a moment, I'm lost in the sensation. But then I remember what I'm here for, and I pull away, breaking the link between us, noting the frustration written across his face.

"It's not safe," I say, my voice low with apology. "Not until I've finished."

Ferran nods, his eyes darkened by desire.

"Get on the bench," I say to him as I prepare my needles. My intention is to draw a set of manacles on the beast that I've already marked him with, essentially binding the creature to him. The root of the herb I used in the ink will also aid in controlling the curse, but it's a risky move, and the weight of this responsibility squats heavily on my shoulders.

Ferran climbs onto the bench, the tendons in his neck tense with stress. I take a deep breath and work quickly and efficiently, trying to detach myself from the process. The needles pierce his skin, fusing the binding tattoo onto his flesh.

When I'm finished, I step back to admire my work. The manacles are intricate, weaving in and out of each other in a complex pattern that I hope is enough. Thanks to an infusion of moon root, they glow faintly on his skin.

He watches me expectantly, and I could tell him I'm done, but I don't want him to leave just yet. I touch him gently on the stomach as his muscles flex under my fingers.

"I miss you," I whisper, walking my fingers lower, but he catches my wrist just as they're about to dip below his waistband.

"I miss you, too," he says, his voice all jagged edges.

I bite my bottom lip and then lean forward so our faces are inches apart. He doesn't stop me as my hand slides into his pants, where I start to stroke his already hardening cock. His breath catches in his throat, and his body shudders on a long exhale.

"Ves," he whispers, and I silence him with a finger pressed to his lips.

"I need to touch you."

My hand continues to pump him, every tug pulling a soft moan from his throat. His hips begin to move, his cock pushing into my hand, seeking more. I love watching him like this.

He's hard and thick, and I feel every rigid vein as his back bows against the bench. One of his hands grips the back of my thigh, his fingers digging into the soft flesh at the crease. After a few more strokes, he moans just as I feel him thicken, and a hot, warm flood covers my hand.

He breathes heavily, a sheen of sweat coating his bare chest. I kiss him gently on the forehead before slowly withdrawing my hand. Our eyes lock, and we remain silent until I finally force myself to look away. If I figure this out, there will be plenty of time for more later.

"We weren't supposed to be doing this," he says as I reach for a cloth to clean both of us up.

I laugh. "Sorry. I couldn't help myself."

He quirks up a brow. "Trust me, you don't need to apologize."

I start to tidy up my supplies.

"Are we done?" he asks, and I nod, suddenly unable to look at him. "What's wrong?"

I pick up a vial and clasp it to my chest before I look over.

"I need to tell you…"

My words drop off.

"What?" Ferran sits up, concern furrowing his brow. "What is it?"

I wave at him, at the newly added cuffs that shimmer on his skin.

"I think it will work." My gaze meets his.

"But?"

"But...I can't be one hundred percent sure." I let those words settle for a moment, giving him a second to catch up to what I'm having trouble articulating.

"And that means we only get one shot at this," he finally says.

"And if I'm wrong..."

"What are the odds you're wrong, Ves?" His expression is all seriousness now.

I shake my head and stride over to my worktable on the far side of the room, slowly rearranging items while I figure out how to answer. Then I look up.

"With everything I've learned about your curse, I'd estimate there's a ninety-five percent chance it will work."

"Ninety-five," he repeats, his hands clenching against the side of the bench.

"Yes."

"Is there anything you can do to make it a hundred?" he asks, but we already both know the answer.

"The only way to do it would be for me to bind myself to you forever."

His gaze meets mine. "So then let's do that. I love you, and I want to be with you."

"I can't," I whisper, trembling with the memories of

my past and what King Malakar did to me. Of what I did in his name because I bound myself to him. "I can't. I swore I'd never do that again, even for you."

"But..." He stops and shakes his head, spitting out a sound of frustration. "No. You're right. I can't ask that of you."

His jaw clenches as he stares at me, his hands still gripped against the table so hard that his knuckles are turning white.

"What if we're just together but never kiss?" he asks, voicing the question I've asked myself a thousand times already.

"Is that what you want?" I ask.

"Not really," he admits. "I want all of you."

"It's too big a risk," I say. "It would be too easy to slip up during a spontaneous moment. It's all I can do to stop myself when you're simply standing in front of me. What about when we're intimate? It will always be a taint on our lives. As much as I want to be together, I can't ask you to risk everything for me. It will haunt you to the end of your days. It's not worth it."

He opens his mouth and then closes it.

"You have good control over your beast now," I say softly.

"But it's not perfect."

"No, but you'll manage much better than you did before. I think it's time for me to leave. I've done everything I can. The rest is up to you."

The words land between us on the hard stone floor like a wet paper bag collapsing under its weight. I can tell he wants to argue, but his shoulders simply drop, like he's been drained of every spark of life.

"Thank you," he says, his voice low. "For everything you've done. I never deserved your help."

I let out a small, dry laugh. "That's not true. It was a pleasure to help you. To try and serve you. My king."

His gaze flashes to me, something inscrutable in it. "I'm leaving tonight," I add. "I've already arranged it."

We just stare at one another, the silence in the room as heavy as a ceiling of stone.

"Very well," he says, pushing himself up and striding out of the room without another word.

Chapter Twenty

The bell hanging over my shop door rings again, and I glance towards the entrance. The apothecary is full, thanks to a steady stream of people coming in and out all day. Everyone's been desperate for my cures, and if I wasn't so damn heartbroken, it might almost be touching that they need me so much.

I look over to see it's Charles Eben, the scholar with the sick son who ratted me out to the king. The circles under his eyes have grown darker, and he's lost weight since I've been gone.

"Everyone out of the way," I call to the milling crowd. "Let him through."

Charles shuffles towards me, and I watch him with my hands planted on my hips, an eyebrow arched. When he reaches the front, he looks up at me with a trepidatious expression. The store is crowded and noisy, and I lean forward, crooking my finger for him to come closer.

He leans in.

"What exactly did you think would happen if you told the king who I was?" I ask. "Did you think he'd leave me here in peace to brew medicine for your boy?"

Charles blinks back a sheen of tears. "I'm sorry," he says. "I didn't know—"

I wave a hand, cutting him off. I'm not actually interested in his explanations. It doesn't matter that he told Ferran. In the end, I should probably be thanking him. Despite the gaping hole currently living in the middle of my chest, I regret nothing about our time together.

"It's fine," I say. "But next time you get the urge to spill a woman's secrets, keep your trap shut. Understood?"

He nods, clutching his hands as I reach under the counter, pull out a bottle, and hand it to him.

"Take this home," I say, offering him the medicine for his son. "He must need it very much by now."

Charles accepts the vial like it's a holy relic between his hands. "Thank you," he croaks. "I'm so sorry again."

"Get out of here," I wave. I don't charge him—there's no need anymore. Ferran made good on his promise, and I am now a very wealthy witch. I've decided I'll continue providing medicine for free for as long as I can afford it. As for that quiet house in the woods, I received a note written in his hand that all I had to do was say the word, and he'd see to it immediately.

I think I'll ask for a castle, though. A big one.

As I move on to the next customer, I try to push thoughts of him away. I don't know if I'll ever send word because that would mean an intense desire to see him, and if I see him again, I might crack. I can't allow myself to be bound to him, and we can't risk breaking the curse. There is no choice left for us.

I spend the rest of the day catching up on my remedies, thankfully too absorbed in my work to give Ferran much thought.

Finally, long after the sun sets, the apothecary has quieted, with just the last few customers left to tend. My bell rings again, and Savryn enters, looking as brawny and gorgeous as always.

When he catches my eye, his face breaks into a huge grin, and I try to summon the appropriate enthusiasm, but I can already tell things are never going to be the same with us.

Ferran is the only man I want. Maybe in time, that will change, but for now, he fills every thread in my heart.

I give Savryn a small smile and then tend to my last few customers while he waits at the far end of the counter, leaning against it with his elbow planted on the surface. He makes small talk with the remaining people in the shop until, finally, everyone leaves.

After following the last person out, I lock the door

before I peer out the window. I've been avoiding the sight all day, but now, I stop to look up at the king's castle perched on top of that ominous, skull-carved mountain.

I wonder what he's doing right now. Is he planning to go into the forest tonight? Will he be able to contain the beast without my help?

"Are you okay?" Savryn asks as he approaches from behind, sliding his arms around my waist. "I've been so worried about you."

My forehead tips against the doorframe as I suck in a deep breath.

"I don't know."

"Where have you been, Ves?" He pulls me in closer, and I know what he wants, but I am not the woman to give it to him anymore.

Gently, I pry his hands away from my stomach and unwrap myself from his hold before I turn around to face him.

"I was with the Feral King," I say as a confused line forms between his brows. I haven't scolded him for blabbing to Charles about my secrets, and there's little point in that now. What's done is done, and I know Savryn didn't set out to hurt me. I give him the abbreviated version of events in the castle, including what happened with Ferran.

When I'm done talking, Savryn takes my hand and presses his mouth to my knuckles.

"You fell in love, Ves?"

There's no jealousy or possessiveness in the statement. If anything, he sounds happy about it. I'd feel the same if he'd told me he met someone, too. That's never what we've been about.

"I guess I did," I say. "Like a complete fool."

Savryn shakes his head. "I don't understand. Then why did you leave?"

I let out a deep sigh. How do I explain why? Savryn doesn't know of my past and why I can't bind myself to Ferran, nor do I want to enlighten him.

"Because the village needed me," I say, and he frowns.

"You could do both. It's not that far."

He's right. It's a weak excuse, but it's all I have right now. "I don't really want to talk about it," I say. "I'd like to just go to bed."

He nods and peers at me before pulling me forward and wrapping me in an embrace. There's nothing suggestive about it. It's the comforting hug of a friend.

"I know we've always had an unconventional sort of relationship, but never doubt that I've always cared about you. You pretend not to care, but I know you do, and you deserve every bit of happiness this world has to offer."

His words make tears burn in my eyes, and one slips down my cheek as I squeeze him. "Thanks, Sav." It's maybe the most articulate thing I've ever heard him say. "I'm lucky to have you."

He pulls back and wraps his hands around my shoulders. "You do have me. No matter what happens, you do. I hate to see you cry."

He rubs a thumb against my cheek, wiping away a tear. Savryn then gives me one last quick hug before unlocking the door to my shop and opening it before he looks back at me.

"I hope you two can work it out. He'd be lucky to have you. Night, Ves."

After Savryn leaves, I lock the door behind him and peer out into the street again. Windows glow in the castle on the cliff, and I wonder if I can make out the solarium where Ferran loves to sit. Better yet, I wonder which window houses my workshop, where we shared so many moments.

But there's no use torturing myself like this. Maybe I should leave Twilight's End after all. Being so close and yet so far is wreaking too much havoc on my heart. Maybe it will hurt less over time.

After one last look outside, I dim the lights and head upstairs to sleep alone in my quiet shop.

Chapter Twenty-One

Over the next few months, I settle back into my routine. Throwing myself into work is the only way to keep the thoughts of Ferran from creeping in and consuming me. The only way to dull the edges of the jagged hole in my chest. It's all just a bandage, though. The pain is still there, growing and spreading. I thought it might recede the longer I was away, but so far, that's just been wishful thinking.

It doesn't help that I hear him at night. Lying in bed, I touch myself listening to his howls in the distance as he hunts the Shadow Demons prowling the border.

I imagine his cries sound more anguished than before, but I don't know if I'm imagining things. What am I hoping for, anyway? That he risks breaking the curse and chooses me over his people? I can't let him do that. I *won't* let him do that.

Along with burying myself in tasks at the apothecary, I've also been perusing my many books on magic, hoping there's some way to guarantee the curse won't break if he kisses me.

My reading suggests the key is him. Until he has absolute control over the beast, he won't be able to hang on to it. I remember his words in the dining room that night: *No magic in the world is strong enough to fight this weakness within me.*

Maybe he understood it all along.

If that's true, that task is up to him now, and there's nothing more I can do to help him. I fear that, no matter what, there will always be a part of him that lives on the edge, and I refuse to tell him this could be the answer. I know he'll only blame himself forever if he can't do what's needed.

Maybe, in time—no. There's no use hoping. I decide maybe I will take him up on that offer of a house in the woods after all and ensure it's far, far away. What I need is distance.

After another busy day in my shop, I sit alone at the counter, listening to the silence. Sifting through the mail that arrived earlier today, I see there's a letter from Celeste. I smile because this is one of the few pieces of happiness I cling to. Once I left the castle, Ferran followed through on his promise to set her up for life. We've been exchanging weekly letters, and she's now married to her sweetheart, building a house where they can spend their days together.

I open her letter, thrilled to find out she's pregnant with their first child. As a wayward tear slips down my cheek, I decide I'll visit her when she's due, just so I can be there to help if there are any complications—plus, I miss her.

While I wallow in my malaise, Savryn comes to see me every day after he's finished hunting. I'm no longer interested in sex, but he seems content enough just to be my friend. He hasn't returned this evening yet unless he was so tired that he just went straight home. I'll check on him tomorrow.

I get up to lock the door and stare up at the Feral King's castle like I do every night, wondering what Ferran is doing and how he's managing with his beast. There haven't been any reports of villager deaths at his hands, so I assume he must be doing well enough.

After a heavy sigh, I dim the lights and trudge up to my room, which has felt so cold and empty ever since I returned from the castle. I used to love coming up here at the end of a busy day, falling onto my plush bed, and snuggling into the blankets, sometimes drawing myself a bath and pouring a glass of wine as I stared out the window.

One souvenir I took from the castle was the book *The King and His Captive*, and I've read it so many times that the spine is starting to fall apart. Celeste insisted I keep it as a memory of our time together.

Not bothering with a bath tonight, I slip into a comfortable pair of leggings and a tunic, dragging *The King and His Captive* with me under the covers, hoping to lose myself in the familiar pages.

I'm not sure how much time passes before howls in the distance disrupt me during one of my favorite scenes —the moment the king is about to fuck his now *very willing* captive bent over a table. I look up. Ferran is out hunting tonight. The hot burn of tears stings my eyes, and I wipe them with the back of my hand. When did I start crying so much?

Lying back on the pillow, I listen to him in the forest, the sound moving away and then getting closer. And closer.

Closer.

Too close.

I sit up.

That's when the screaming starts.

Before I know what I'm doing, I'm tripping down the stairs, flinging open the door to my shop, and running into the street. Another shriek comes from the end of the road, and then I see him.

Ferran stands at the edge of the village in his beast form. Huddled along the buildings are dozens of villagers in their night clothes, and I want to shout at them for coming outside. Why didn't they just stay safe in their homes? How foolish can they be?

Ferran takes a slow step forward, accompanied by more terrified screams.

"Ferran!" I call, and his head turns slowly towards me.

I wish I were still tethered to him so I could sense what's happening in his thoughts. How close to the edge is he? He takes another step, prowling through the village on his silent, pawed feet.

More villagers spill out of their homes, arriving to see what all the fuss is about, and I start yelling at them. "Go back inside!" They pay me no mind as they stand there trembling, watching Ferran take another step.

My chest crumples as I watch him. If I thought he'd ever gain complete control over the beast, this moment proves that's only ever going to be a dream. It's clear some part of him will always remain wild and impossible to leash.

The village whips into a combination of wild terror and silent horror as Ferran continues down the street. A group of men gather behind him, clutching the modest weapons of farmers and merchants—jeweled daggers and the occasional sword meant to hang over the fireplace, along with shovels and pickaxes.

I have to get him out of here before he does something he will live to regret before they get it in their heads to attack. I can't let a fight break out; they won't stand a chance against him.

"Ferran," I scream again, this time waving my arms as though he can't see me perfectly clearly where I'm standing. "You have to control it."

He blinks, his dark eyes glowing in the moonlight with slivers of yellow, and then cricks his neck before he takes another step.

"Don't touch him!" I yell at the villagers. "I'll get him out of here." They exchange wary glances, clearly not sure if they should trust me. "Please. I won't let him hurt any of you."

They hesitate as I stand in the middle of the road, staring at me like I've completely lost my mind. They all believe I'm the village healer. How am *I* going to protect them?

Ferran takes another slow step, his fang-filled mouth stretching to show off pointed teeth glinting in the light of the stars as more panicked screams fill the air.

And then, Ferran lunges.

Chapter Twenty-Two

A scream tears from my throat, terrified he's about to rip apart some poor villager.

But he's not heading for any of them.

Quickly, I realize he's heading for me.

His massive form pounces, landing in front of me in a cloud of dust before I'm scooped up and tossed over his massive shoulder. I could stop him, but I don't want to hurt him, and I'm still pretending I'm something else to these villagers. I don't want any of them to know what I truly am, though perhaps I've blown a bit of my cover with my attempts to stop Ferran tonight.

Before I can give it too much thought, Ferran is bounding away from the village, and then we're in the forest, trees blurring past my vision. Now that we have no witnesses, I could use my magic, but I wait, wondering what he'll do. In all our experiments, it was never me his beast lunged for. I always assumed it was some deep-seated instinct that understood I was the apex predator, forcing his beast to go for more helpless prey.

Suddenly, we come to a stop, and Ferran hauls me off his shoulder, placing me on the ground just as he shifts. Then, he's standing in front of me in all his raw male glory, looking wild and free.

The last thing I expect to see is the massive smile on his face.

"I did it!" he yells, his fist raising in the air. "I did it!"

"You did what?" I ask.

He wraps his hands around my shoulders. "I was testing myself. Could I walk through the village and control myself? And I did it, Ves. Your spells worked."

It takes me a moment to process his words. He controlled it. There, in the middle of a village full of humans, he controlled the beast. He's smiling so broadly that his eyes sparkle, and he might be the most beautiful man I've ever seen.

"You did that," I say, catching his enthusiasm. "You did that! Ferran, you did it! You learned to control it."

"I did. I've been practicing every free moment since you left, and I was sure this was the final test. It's mine now, and I understand how to tame it, how to use it. How to make it mine."

I listen to him, marveling at his words. At his control. At his strength.

"Why are you crying?" he asks, and sure enough, my face is wet with tears.

"I've missed you so much," I say with a sob.

He pulls me to him, and I wrap my arms around his waist, burying my face in his warm chest. He smells so good, like the reminder of so many things I want to hold on to forever.

"Gods, I've missed you too, Ves. You have no idea how hard I've had to hold myself back every single fucking day from coming here and finding you. I've been miserable."

"Me too," I whisper.

"I came tonight because I wanted you to see. I wanted you to be proud of me."

I sniffle. "I'm so proud of you, Ferran. You have no idea."

He tips up my chin. "I want to kiss you now more than I've ever wanted anything." The words are sad, pulled thin like strands of melting sugar.

I open my mouth and then close it, unsure if I should reveal the knowledge that has been plaguing my thoughts.

But he controlled it. What if this is the answer?

"What is it?" he asks.

"I might have found a way for you to stop the curse from breaking if you kiss me."

"What?" he asks again, instantly on alert. "I'll do whatever it is."

"I've been doing a lot of reading, and I think the key is

you. You're the only one who can effectively tie it to yourself, but only if you have complete control over the monster within you."

I let him process that for a moment. "You mean like I just did."

"Yes. Like that."

He pauses, considering those words.

"Do you trust yourself, Ferran?"

He swallows. "I think so. Gods, I want to so much."

I take his face in my hands. "You can do this. I believe in you. Start slowly. Just think about keeping the beast within you. Don't let it go."

He nods, his hands clamping around my waist as he pulls me towards him. "I can do this. For you. For us."

"For you, too."

"Definitely for me," he answers, the corner of his mouth crooking into a smile as he leans in. His lips touch mine, feather-light at first, and shock courses through me, spreading through my arms and legs, filling that hole in my chest I've been carrying around like a dead weight. His lips are warm and soft but firm at the same time.

"Open your mouth," he growls, and his tongue slips between my teeth to touch mine. I moan as he pulls me in closer, and this is the most decadent kiss I've ever experienced. After a moment, he pulls away, his eyes wide as he stares at me.

"How do you feel?" I ask tentatively.

He looks down at himself and then back up.

"It's still there. My beast is still there."

That's when I break into a grin. "You did it."

"*We* did it," he says, and then he's kissing me again, his mouth crashing into mine.

The kiss deepens as Ferran's hands quest over my body, touching me everywhere. His tongue explores every inch of my mouth. He lets out a snarl that feels like his beast, pulsing with power, but he restrains it, holding it at bay.

We move together, our bodies writhing as our hands roam up and down, the heat between us growing. I can't get enough of him. I want to feel him, touch him, taste him.

"Take me," I whisper, and he doesn't hesitate. Ferran lifts me up, our lips still locked, and carries me to a nearby tree. He leans me against it, and I wrap my legs around his waist, pulling him closer. His hands dig into my thighs in exactly the way I pictured the first day I met him. Firm and possessive.

He starts to kiss my neck, his hands gripping my ass as I let out soft moans. The rough bark of the tree presses against my back, reminding me that after months of living like a ghost, I've finally come back to life.

His hard cock presses against my aching pussy, needing him and wanting him so much. I've been on the edge every moment, thinking about him, wanting him. I use a bit of magic to do away with the barrier of my leggings, shredding them apart.

"Fuck, that's a handy talent," Ferran breathes, and then he's lining himself up with my entrance. "I'm going to fuck you so thoroughly, you'll forget we were ever apart," he growls, and then he enters me in a single, powerful thrust. A loud moan escapes my lips as his cock fills me up, stretching me open. I grip his biceps as an anchor as he plunges into me over and over again.

"I love you, Vespera," he whispers into my ear, and I pull his face to mine.

"I've missed you so much."

"I want to hear you moan. Tell me you want me to fuck you," he says, and I can feel him growing harder and thicker inside me.

"Oh, goddess. I want you to fuck me, Ferran."

He reaches down and pushes his thumb against my clit, sending a wave of pleasure washing over me. I scream out as my walls clench tightly around his cock, keeping him locked in place deep inside me, where I'll hang on to him for eternity.

"That's right. Scream for me, beautiful witch. You're mine now. Mine forever."

"Please don't stop," I beg, and then he's fucking me harder, faster, his hips slapping against mine, his fingers digging into my flesh. I'm falling apart, losing my mind, and all I want is for this to last forever.

"You feel so good, Ves." He leans in and nips my ear,

sending a shiver down my spine, and then my orgasm crashes over me.

I cry out, clinging to him as he continues to push into me, his movements becoming erratic. Then, his cock twitches as he groans, filling me with the warmth of his release. I wrap my arms around his neck as our lips collide in a hungry kiss that is more than just a kiss.

It's a promise and a vow.

Because this kiss nearly cost us both everything.

"I love you," Ferran whispers, his forehead pressed to mine.

"I love you so much," I whisper back. "Take me back to my shop. You're spending the night with me."

He grins and pulls me away from the tree, keeping me wrapped in his arms. "Whatever you wish."

He carries me back towards the now-silent village, our mouths locked together. Thankfully, everyone has retreated into their homes because Ferran is naked, and I'm not wearing any pants. Not that I really care if anyone sees it, but the people of this village are easily scandalized.

We maneuver inside the apothecary, and he takes a moment to look around.

"This is really nice," he says, and I huff out a laugh.

"Not like my workshop in the castle."

He looks at me. "What do you want to do?"

"What do you mean?"

"Live here? How will you help the villagers?"

I think of what Savryn said to me. How it really wasn't far at all between here and the castle.

"I think we can work it out," I say. "Maybe I'll open a second location in the castle. People can come to see me there, too."

He raises an eyebrow, and I direct him to my bedroom upstairs.

"You really think anyone will come to the Feral King's castle for a healing tonic?"

He lays me on the bed and then crawls over me, his body hovering over mine.

"I've been thinking about that," I say. "I think it's time for the Feral King to adopt a new image. One that speaks to the brave, strong king who has done everything in his power to protect his people."

He gives me a small smile. "I like the sounds of that."

"Then kiss me," I whisper. "Kiss me like you mean it."

And then, he does.

Receive the latest updates about new releases, ARCs, bonus content, and more when you sign up for my newsletter at nishajtuli.com.

Also by Nisha

Artefacts of Ouranos
    Trial of the Sun Queen
    Rule of the Aurora King
    Fate of the Sun King

Nightfire Quartet
    Heart of Night and Fire
    Dance of Stars and Ashes
    Storm of Ink and Blood

Cursed Captors
    Wicked is the Reaper
    Feral is the Beast

To Wake a Kingdom

About Nisha

Nisha has always been obsessed with worlds she cannot see. From Florin to Prythian, give her a feisty heroine, a windswept castle, and true love's kiss, and she'll be lost in the pages forever. Bonus points for protagonists slaying dragons in kick-ass outfits.

When Nisha isn't writing, it's usually because one of her two kids needs something (she loves them anyway). After they're finally in bed, she'll usually be found with her e-reader or knitting sweaters and scarves, perfect for surviving a Canadian winter.

Follow for More:

Website: http://nishajtuli.com/
TikTok: https://www.tiktok.com/@nishajtwrites
Instagram: https://www.instagram.com/nishajtwrites/

Printed in Poland
by Amazon Fulfillment
Poland Sp. z o.o., Wrocław

34709157R00106